Nights at the Embassy

by the same author

Nights at the Embassy

stories by
Elizabeth Smither

Auckland University Press

First published 1990
Auckland University Press
University of Auckland
Private Bag
Auckland

ISBN 1 86940 051 8

Typeset by Toptype

Printed in Hong Kong

Publication assisted by the Literature Committee
of the Queen Elizabeth II Arts Council

for Fiona

Acknowledgement is made to the publishers of the books and journals where some of these stories first appeared. 'The Girl Who Loved Mathematics' was previously published in the *Evening Standard,* and in *New Women's Fiction 2,* edited by Aorewa McLeod and published by New Women's Press; 'Shakespeare & Co.' appeared in *Woman-sight*, edited by Suzann Olsson and published by Nagare Press, and in the *London Magazine*; 'The Love of One Orange' appeared in *New Women's Fiction 1*, edited by Cathie Dunsford and published by New Women's Press; 'Librarians' appeared in *Descant* (Toronto) and in the *Listener*; and 'Nights at the Embassy' in *Landfall*.

Contents

Shakespeare & Co. ❧

What was the name of Elizabeth Browning's dog? was almost the only answer I got that night. **Flush.** And even then, in spite of the triumphant sound, it didn't fall into the circle with any recognition. The others immediately began questioning whether it was a spaniel or a red setter. What sort of dog would spend most of its time forgoing walks, under a sickbed? Was I sure? Did **Flush** refer to a temperature?

I was sitting on a cane chair in the front room of my publisher's house, a chair from which I might have leapt metaphorically with obscure answers. **In what street was Sylvia Beach's bookshop situated?**

But the other guests were doing well. There was a very pretty woman with red hair and a flowing dress whom I had thought of no consequence: she had confidently given the year of **Victor Hugo**'s birth. And my publisher, also a source of chagrin, though I couldn't explain to myself why this should be so — surely one wanted a well-read publisher? — glibly gave the most famous translator of **Colette.**

The room had heavy old-fashioned venetians and I thought this made matters worse: black or white, light or shade, seemed to be cast on us. A heavy shower was falling, which was the reason, since departure was delayed, for starting the game. Otherwise we might have played Scrabble, which at least moved the hands, or gone on discussing the subject which had preoccupied us at dinner: the new tax laws and then, though how this was a consequence I remained uncertain, how 'colonial' remains a tainted word to the European.

'**Henry James. 1881**,' said the red-haired woman to a question that had given a plot summary of **Portrait of a Lady: a study of American virtue versus European sophistication set in Rome.**

'Wonderful,' the publisher called and the woman, whose name was Nina, tucked her legs under her on the window seat and stretched her neck so it was resting on a small cushion.

'It's all very well for you antipodeans,' the second man, an Englishman, exclaimed. 'I've got a feeling you've been cramming.'

'Come now,' the publisher replied. 'It's your home ground. Or your fair cousins'. **Melville, James, and the poet who leapt off Brooklyn Bridge**.'

'**Virginia Woolf** walking with the stones in her pocket to the River Ouse,' I heard myself saying with a voice like **Alice**, coming from a well. 'Do you think she changed cardigans to one with pockets? Or weighed the stones first on scales?' I had a persistent view of her in russet: a loose cardigan with a knitted belt to pull close like arms.

The Waves had come and gone and I was waiting for **Orlando**. **Sissinghurst**, I said to myself: the all-white garden. Nothing all black. No one would ask about the Boston Red Sox either. Perhaps **Sylvia Beach** did not know of them.

The publisher brought two more bottles of wine out, holding them by the necks, a Pouilly-Fuissé and a Nuits-St-Georges. I felt suddenly cheerful, having something to blame for my poor showing.

'Here's to **Flush**, my one correct answer,' I said, deciding to go public. I was taking a risk the publisher would not withdraw his contract. 'Are there any more about dogs?'

'**Literary figures who were famous Dreyfusards?**'
'**Hugo? the de Goncourts . . .?**'
'Give three, it says.'

It was still raining and the room had grown darker. A famous writer had told me she wrote better when drunk. How many of these tragic dates were lubricated?

The publisher lived in a suburb that was like an island: reached by ferry it seemed to have a distinct vegetation, even an architecture of its own. The ferry buildings on both sides were dilapidated, little better than abandoned hangars: they seemed to increase the excitement of a visit. The floors of these hangars always seemed to be wet and glistening and in one I had a recollection of half-buried rails. The ferry, for years almost as battered as the terminals, had been refurbished to make it a tourist attraction: a tiny bar was hung with nets and glass floats, dried swordfish.

Sometimes I sat on the port side, eating a cheese roll, slightly stale, as the ferry slipped clear of the piers and headed for the open sea. Though the corresponding terminus could be dimly seen, the cheese roll and the wash, so like voracious appetite, induced a feeling of melancholy. The sea gave no answers but it sent out endless questions: **The name of the tubercular girl who upset John Keats on the voyage to Naples? Three ships associated with Herman Melville?**

The publisher was waiting, standing by his white car, at the exit. Behind his shoulder rose a substantial white hotel with palm trees at intervals. I had taken the precaution of wiping the cheese crumbs from my mouth: authors owed it to themselves to look hungry. Sometimes we stopped at another hotel for a drink: it took two gins to overcome my fear that this was an economy version of the business-lunch-with-rejection but it turned out, since my royalties were small, the publisher wanted to sympathise. I refused a third gin, fearing I might emulate the hysterical behaviour of Americans at the New York docks who called up for news of **Little Nell.**

'You should ask for an advance', more experienced authors advised. 'Demand to know your sales, first translation rights.' One publisher kept a blackboard which the telephonist would consult. I wondered if **Sylvia Beach** kept a slate against **Ulysses**. I imagined **Norah Barnacle** approaching in a suit with padded shoulders, carrying a flat-bottomed willow basket. Quickly to my mental picture of **Shakespeare & Co**. I added a trapdoor through which **Sylvia**, bravely hoarding prisoners of war as well as first editions, could escape.

The publisher's wife was in Rheims, completing a study of **Racine**. Her accent was pure, though she thought of it as only mimicry. It was based on precise English vowels which had often crossed the Channel: the light transfer of huge tracts of land. Anjou and Poitou looked and spelt like large, badly wrapped parcels. Louise lived in a tiny flat under a desirable (to my eyes) mansard roof, carefully counting her francs into small piles for milk, the Métro, a weekly, closely written aerogramme. Her cooking was rudimentary and frugal: the same teabag was put out to dry like a herring: it gave two demi-tasses of equal-coloured but not quite equal-flavoured water. One evening, dunking it for the second time in fiercely boiling water, Louise thought how odd it was that the Russians with their comfortable samovars set such store by French phrases in conversation. Somehow the realisation made her homesick.

Once a week, on Fridays, Louise ate at a tiny brasserie where the waiter, sensing perhaps some mystery about her, was beginning to unbend. But in a year of Fridays she knew she could never earn her own table. For the rest of the week her staple was a mildly scented garlic salami, cheap and probably despised by the French, which she prepared in a variety of ways. Sometimes thin slices vanished between layers of sliced potato enlivened with onion, the whole welded together with potato-thickened milk. Quite often, though she thought of some delicious variation, like variations in the translation of a word, her energy dissipated as soon as she left the Métro. She drank a glass of cold milk, looking over the rooftops and made a sandwich of salami and tomatoes. Her professor found her hardworking, charming, but no one in her advanced class offered any social life.

'If only Louise was here she would get this: **A French *fin de siècle* novel that begins with a description of miniature liqueurs?'**

'How *is* Louise?' the woman in the window seat asked. She was lying on her side, smoking.

'I guess,' the publisher said, consulting his watch, but perhaps without comprehending, or, after such a long absence it might have been automatic, 'she is sleeping.' For some reason he imagined a threadbare, over-laundered, cotton eiderdown of the sort used in hospitals. Surprisingly, he was not far from the truth.

'Is anyone else influenced by food in books?' I asked.

I could recall boiling quantities of plain rice when reading Naipaul, even looking around for brass dishes, which of course I did not possess. Lorna Doone influenced me towards bacon and apples. Moravia always made me feel like pasta.

'The **Lucia** novels often made me feel like toast,' Nina said. 'But of course you could say the same of **Anita Brookner** or **Barbara Pym**. Convalescent novels.'

'I suppose one could distinguish,' the Englishman

objected, seeing a national dish was almost at stake. 'Cinnamon toast for **Pym** and French toast for **Brookner**.'

'Very droll,' said the publisher. 'I think the answer we are looking for is **Huysmans**.'

The room was so full of smoke my eyes were beginning to water.

I had once come back on the ferry — the publisher's evenings always ended sedately by car — and had to jump. It had been a sharp lesson in literary distinction. A friend and I had lingered in a little all-night café not far from the second terminal and then forgotten the time. This friend had a penchant for evening dress; I had borrowed a long velvet screen-printed gown with a hood. Invariably when we dressed up, our hosts had dressed down and the evening never quite 'took'. To the surly man, ignoring our pleas to bring the ferry closer, we were snobs who deserved to spend the night shivering in the terminal, our feet tucked up on benches, inspected by wharf rats. Being dressed as **Madame de Montespan** and **George Sand** had made it impossible to reveal ourselves as hardworking mothers who mostly wore yellow rubber gloves. Another friend who was a Lady Lion had been forced to resuscitate a road accident victim while wearing a flimsy Greek tunic; her husband, the Lion, stood beside her holding a cardboard spear. I looked at the Englishman who had dangerously mixed his drinks and thought I spied the disguise of the **Scarlet Pimpernel:** the drooping lids and port-flushed cheeks of **Sir Percy Blakeney**.

'Twenty-six questions attempted; ten certain; twenty-four to go. I feel a disgrace to my profession,' said the publisher.

But we all hastened to reassure him: the Englishman who worked for a rival firm, but one without a branch in this country, spoke of his having, even in trade circles, a nose like a wine connoisseur. I hastened to agree, since he had risked my first, profitless novel. Nina in the window seat smiled enigmatically and extolled his cooking abilities, though she had brought dessert.

'Besides, you did best,' I protested. 'I only got **Flush** but you knew who the **White Rabbit** was modelled on, the year **Hart Crane** jumped, **Balzac**'s favourite mistress.'

'And what laid **James Joyce** low and where.'

'I got the hospital wrong and the date.'

'Surely only **Sylvia Beach** would care.'

It has always puzzled me that the scenes of deep passions or reveries are unchanged by our heightened moments in them. Certain streets, views, rooms, should be bathed in a different light. But not the light of quizzes. That penetrating exactness that was summed up in some fatuous articles with a biblical flavour: In (**year**) (**author's name**) published (**name of article**) in (**name of magazine**). It was usually in the form of a calendar and embellished with 'a six-week visit to Tangiers', 'three months' intensive writing (**Rilke**) in a castle.' No mention of days of grippe (depending on the century), nights of cocottes, the MS (final draft) left on a train. Weren't these questions, to excuse our failure, the same thing? Would the authors have recognised them?

The gap between author and publisher had become clear to me in the foyer of a luxury hotel in Toronto. The authors at the festival could not quite manage to blend with the guests. Late one afternoon as we were waiting for drinks, a bride suddenly appeared, like **The Woman in White**, pressing her veil against the wide glass doors. Behind her walked the groom and a remarkable wedding party: men in tails and women in silks and pillbox hats, some with a feather. As they parted our little party, an Israeli author, greatly honoured in his country, intimated he saw signs of divorce. His black jersey, like all our secret writing clothes, was festooned with lint.

'If someone started a **Shakespeare & Co** here, what would they call it? **Sargeson & Co? Shadbolt & Co?**'

'How about Sobriety & Co?'

In honour of **Huysmans** the publisher had brought out the Drambuie and Armagnac.

'I believe you have published a book?' the Englishman said politely, now the quiz was abandoned.

'I'll give you a copy, if you like,' the publisher said. I suspected he had a store.

How soothing and well-balanced liqueurs are, I thought. So many brain cells are failing, flailing, yet they bring a balance. It seemed miraculous that this could be applied externally. Under the influence of liqueurs one could almost belong to two political parties at once.

But when I came to inscribe my name I couldn't seem to control the pen. The top of my head felt cold, detached, like an egg that has been decapitated. I tried once on the title page and again near the imprint.

'Don't worry. That will do. I expect we are all too befuddled to go on with the quiz.'

'Too colonial, perhaps,' I said, not sure whether I meant to sound wistful or ironic.

The publisher drove the Englishman and myself over the bridge and through the suburbs with what seemed like excessive care. When we came to my apartment and they handed me out and we exchanged clumsy embraces — I intended to kiss the **Scarlet Pimpernel** on both cheeks, French-fashion, but I got his ear — I noticed how deep the gutter was, like **Flush** under the bed, and what an effort it required to cross.

The Love of One Orange 🙟

The poet, William Empson, said there were two time scales human beings understood: the momentary and the length of one's life. I think it was a combination of the momentary and the projected length of my life that brought about the death of my first romance.

I was really in love with a man who knew a man who slept with a goat. This man may have been one of his flatmates. He shared an old house, very run down but with a kind of pioneer charm, long lugubrious windows like disapproving eyes, overhanging verandah like a piece of valuable old lace — the drains were like torn edges. There were plenty in the neighbourhood scandalised at the endless procession of young girls who disappeared inside. My mother undertook, on the afternoon I told her I was going there, to tell my father I was returning a book.

There was hardly a book in sight but an old retainer — this seemed the right word for her — called Stevie, whose function was to produce trays of food at parties. The food was pretty inedible with lots of corn and cheese but Stevie's efforts — she was eighty at least and wore heavy makeup — were greeted with great applause. There were two goats on the property; the one that was rumoured to share a bed was probably a ploy to deter marriage-minded girls and lend a raffish charm at the same time. There was also an old car without an engine which was tethered to the nearest lamp-post with a bit of rope.

The man I fell in love with was of course surrounded by

girls and they were all charmed, as I was, by his sorrowing stories of coming from a parsonage family and being the despair of his elderly mother and a 'black sheep'. One of the goats I think was black, as a kind of reinforcement. So in the end I went out, such is the desire to get into combat in love or war, with one of his friends, a man who shared the same office.

> *Oh, life is a glorious cycle of song,*
> *A medley of extemporanea;*
> *And love is a thing that can never go wrong;*
> *And I am Marie of Roumania.*

I swung those days between opposites. My clothing was like that, at one moment a white sheath frock with large roses rambling all over it — it was as painful to walk in as being hobbled by thorns — then a midnight-blue brocade given by a cousin, which I had made to my own design — its short, button-down-the-back jacket had fur at throat and wrist and made me feel very Russian. Long before I met any suitable candidates I was dressed like A Man for All Seasons. There was one spectacular red dress with a wide belt and discreet gathering over the hips which brought a gasp of pleasure from this new date. He must have failed to notice I had on the wrong shoes. This was always happening — I went in so big for outward show I frequently couldn't afford the final touch, silver sandals or red pumps.

This new man, I'll call him A——, expressed some of the bitterness I thought I was concealing at the ring of girls sitting literally at the feet of the man I adored and had dressed especially to see. I was thinking of a walk around the house in the dark where the week before I had been kissed near the chicken coop (empty) by another of the flat mates. Really they should have been called The Four Musketeers because they were so casual and self-supporting about girls. Perhaps they even passed them down the line. It was not a very pleasant kiss and I said something tactless — I was often tactless to hide my inexperience — 'That was very sloppy, J——,' to which he replied 'I don't care' and tried again, just like a man fixing a car with the wrong spanner.

I think I was wearing something understated and demure, as though I had already sensed the competition and wished to stand out. A—— was standing beside me, an amused look on his face, probably about as amused as mine was disdainful. The hero sat in a broken-down armchair with a crescent of upturned and laughing faces about him; only the entrance of Stevie with some unspeakable grilled concoction could compete.

I went outside and stood on the verandah, looking at the moon and the goats. I could see the shape of the car and its bit of frayed rope. It had about one week to go before the Traffic Department discovered it was engineless and took it off to the dump. I half wished I had the nerve to go for a walk in the direction of the chicken house but I didn't. A shape materialised beside me and we fell into conversation. He didn't seem at all interesting, that is until my tendency for opposites got operating; I mainly thought it would be good to be seen with someone if the hero should get up to stretch his legs.

After two dates, during which I got news of the hero — one week he had thrown a bottle of ink at the wall, another time he was suspected of ruining the clutch on an office car, a charge he strenuously denied while admitting he drove like a devil — I began to think I almost preferred shyness since it made me feel bolder. Certainly my clothes, a new maroon skirt — I had read a story about an adulterous affair where the heroine put on a maroon skirt when she was ready — seemed bold against his one dark suit and more casual slacks with a sports jacket. I began to feel sophisticated again and when we went to a dance at a mountain house in midwinter, I put on the red dress with the wide belt that caused the reaction. The floor was pleasantly dusted with talcum powder even if the food was cold and I felt thoroughly Vogue all evening. I told myself I was marking time.

We came down from the mountain house and a horse ran on to the road and collided with the car of one of the jazzmen in the band. The horse had to be put down and the jazzman wore a collar for weeks like a shire horse. Everything seemed scandalous and vaguely exciting, as though we were always in the car behind the President.

I'm not sure when the liking for shyness grew into a settled thing. Love or something like it can easily grow out of being comfortable. All you need to do is up the danger of the world — the horse and jazzman was one example — and comfort seems safe and warm and then intimate. The hero faded a bit or got ink on his feet. There may have been a police raid. Or Stevie died and things weren't the same. I still got news but after a while I began to feel superior to it. I even culled a few things out of my wardrobe, the Russian fur evening suit for one. What it needed was a man in a white suit like David Bowie.

> *Whose love is given over-well*
> *Shall look on Helen's face in hell,*
> *Whilst they whose love is thin and wise*
> *May view John Knox in paradise.*

We went to the movies and we visited friends (his) to

play cards. I didn't care for cards much — I've never had the competitive spirit except for a short time in school sports and over the hero — and I played with a fine carelessness that often caused me to win. I noticed on these occasions A—— expressed an ill-concealed chagrin. I wisecracked a lot — the other couple were rather silent and serious; after four games, of which I usually won two, they would get supper. I often came home with a headache.

One night he brought me flowers in a long box. He had been working late at the office for two weekends; this was a reward for patience. I opened the box in trepidation since I knew the names of few flowers — rose, daisy, dandelion — but they were carnations and I could look sophisticated. What wasn't sophisticated was to think

> *Why is it no one ever sent me yet*
> *One perfect limousine, do you suppose?*
> *Ah no, it's always just my luck to get*
> *One perfect rose.*

I think I was perfectly sweet all evening after that. And Sunday I helped polish up the seats of the Vauxhall with shoe polish.

A—— talked of introducing me to his parents, who lived in another city. I drove past their house in a bus — it looked as though it was made of gingerbread — with ash trees in front of it. I imagined a woman, stocky in a white apron like a Parisian waiter's, with flour-coated hands. I would wear a skirt and blouse, the blouse only slightly transparent. His father would approve of me instantly.

Winter came and each Friday night as I stood at the Children's entrance to the library, seeing the last stragglers off with a cheery 'Goodnight' which quite belied my aching feet but was lightened by the thought of A——'s Vauxhall, which would soon be snaking along into one of the vacant parking spaces — 'a woman who was being collected' — I had a feeling of repleteness, in spite of the fact I could eat a horse. I would linger a few minutes, touching books and straightening the Children's desk, putting a last armful of picture books away or throwing out flowers that would not last the weekend. Half the time I forgot to take any books home for myself. My last extravagant purchase had been a pair of stiletto-heeled American shoes in a rusty colour that I imagined matched my hair. The heels could not be worn in the library because they left dents in the linoleum tiles. I think they were in revenge for all the outfits that never got their proper complement. I put them on just by the door before letting myself out.

Usually when I opened the door of the car, there would be a greeting between casual and shy. In my mind's eye it was not a Vauxhall at all but the car of a Mafia boss and I, teetering on my American four-inch heels, was a mobster's moll. A whole day in a library plays havoc with your fantasies. I would teeter past and then at the last moment turn the handle. But this night there was no greeting but a face straight ahead, watching the windscreen wipers with their characteristic erratic swish-shudder-swish. I sat beside him in silence, stowing my books on the floor, playing with my gloves. Nor did he make any attempt to move off in the direction of a coffee shop.

'I want to explain to you a problem which I've had at the office. I want you to listen carefully without interrupting and then at the end tell me Yes or No. It's a bit technical but I'll simplify it so you'll understand. You don't mind if we sit here for a bit? It's been worrying me all day and if I don't get it off my chest, I won't sleep either.'

I kicked my shoes off, suddenly aware my feet were aching and since we weren't going anywhere, I might as well be comfortable. I was parched for a cup of coffee.

'Fire ahead then. I'll do my best but don't hold it against me if I get it wrong.'

'Any fool would get it right. There's only one feasible solution. At least if I'm right there is. Just listen carefully.'

I lay back against the seat — the seats were fairly dented anyway and my back sank into a hollow. I was all ears. Just the same I had my fingers crossed. He began with a bit of a preamble and straight away I could tell it had as much to do with personalities as design factors. The hero came into it and I realised for the first time they were enemies. But the greatest temptation was not to watch the rain and the wipers. At the best of times I could hardly take my eyes off the drops as they fattened then burst then ran in smears like street lamps. There was no sense of loss though, as another drop was always growing alongside. It reminded me of the First World War.

I became aware of a voice in phrases and snatches. 'If something is designed to . . . and it fits these parameters, then why should it . . .?' He really had no idea how much he was giving away in his factual account. I caught little glimpses of body language too, rigidity and then a leaning gesture, like an overture. He waved his arms about and once he struck his fist into his palm. It certainly wasn't dispassionate. It was about twenty minutes before I was absolutely sure the answer was No. If only he didn't ask me for a recapitulation.

For the rest of the time I watched the raindrops. I figured if he looked at my face, he must think I was concentrating hard. But actually I was just listening with half an ear to the tone that would tell me the story was coming to a close.

Dorothy Dix, I said to myself. Dear Sir, I have carefully considered your problem and advise you to . . . . I must be careful not to say No too quickly. That way it wouldn't look like a guess.

'Well? What do you think? You did manage to follow it?'

'I think I followed it fairly carefully. I'm feeling pretty tired. Just the same it seems obvious to me that the answer I would have to give is No. There is no way the other solution makes any sense. Logically . . .'

But I was cut short. An arm curled around my shoulders and a mouth, guided by glasses, leaned and drank from mine. 'You're really very intelligent, for a girl. I thought you'd see my point. Now how about some coffee?'

We just got there as it closed. The rain was falling steadily now and it seemed senseless to go and park by the sea. A—— confessed he was tired. But he had seats for the Saturday movie.

That night I couldn't sleep. I kept seeing raindrops swelling and bursting. I thought of myself as insincere, taking a short cut that in years to come I would bound to be caught out in. The words of praise could so easily be reversed. Like the Red Baron I had scored once but could I go on scoring? What if I made some inept reference on Saturday that showed I hadn't been listening properly at all.

A——'s left hand snaked along the back of the seat and his right hand lifted his glasses off in a casual motion. The first manoeuvre must have gone back to the Model T or earlier — the chaise longue — the right hand to whoever made the first spectacles. There was something of that time sequence in the two movements — the left hand was so much more assured — the glasses were held up against the dashboard as though A—— contemplated polishing them. He blinked a little, owlishly. He had told me his eyes had been ruined by studying and the corrective glasses hadn't worked. I thought of all my dresses, which had surely brought me to this pass, and wondered how I looked to him.

'When you take your glasses off, what do you see?'

'Do you mean in the street? Well it's a blur, greyish with stripes in it. Gold melting stripes. I know they are the street lights.'

'It must be scary. One minute lights, the next a blur.'

'Not really. I'm used to it.'

'Tell me. When you look at me what do you see?'

'Close up, do you mean?'

'When you're embracing me.'

He gulped a bit then and there was a pause.

'Honestly, I won't be offended.'

'When you're close to me your face reminds me of an orange.'

I had my arms around him quite soon after, as much in comfort as anything, and to hide the mortal wound. The *moment*, as Empson would say. Over his shoulder — he was wearing tweeds that night — I looked at a suburban landscape with the moon floating above it. It was as though I was embracing the moon, not him. Disc to disc. I was closer to the moon.

Later that night I walked up and down in front of my mirror. I used to look at my body when it started to develop and imagine it was a cathedral — Chartres — something anonymous and spiky at the same time. The swellings were growing over the ribs which were flying buttresses. I hated to think of it becoming fat and thick. Now I knew it would, in its most intimate moments, be nothing more than a blur.

I felt very very uneasy. I had nothing against men in glasses

Girls seldom make passes
At men who wear glasses

but it was a shock to discover I looked like an orange. I imagined myself as a raindrop dissolving into a streak, a stain on the bed. In some ways I guessed it might have advantages: A—— would never notice if my makeup was smeared. I would be an orange gasping for breath. I couldn't say why it displeased me so much.

But the second shock — the long question I had correctly answered — was much worse. I couldn't get over the feeling I had cheated and had an unfair advantage. And almost immediately following this success, like a cunning runner who uses a short cut, I felt uneasy and undone. You see, I had made my decision a good twenty minutes before the peroration. In those moments when I marked time I felt both exultation and fear. If A—— hadn't been so tired and relieved to find me complaisant, supportive as well as agreeing, I might have been asked to account for my reasoning. The thought of a life — because the most obtuse person could see this conversation had advanced our courtship several moves — spent in this kind of dissembling made me ache to my bones. Perhaps it would be better to begin with a confession, on our very next date, of my perfidy. Then I could be forgiven, despised probably, and we could begin again.

How it fell apart in the end I am not sure — it is too long ago. It may have been — I think it was something like this — I became extra warm to cover my deficiencies and this displeased; I kissed with more ardour than I should have after a Friday at the library; I longed and hinted I longed to meet his mother. He ceased mentioning his address and after a while I forgot it.

I still used to say my prayers — a routine more than anything, like putting on the short white gloves we wore with everything (except evening dress). Sometimes a small voice, not deep but inclined to be squeaky, told me A—— was wrong for me but I quickly subdued it. Later on of course I was pleased to recognise it as an ally. They say you're saved by what you imitate and if the voice of conscience and reason was a whimper, the voice of Dorothy Parker, except where her verses were two lines long and I reversed them, was strong.

It's funny how actions seem logical a long time later and even then they seem to hang by a thread. At the time I had never heard of Empson, and Time and Space — I still don't know what either term means — will occupy me to the end of my life and longer. But why a moment combined with the intimation of a life should serve to destroy a romance I can't tell. It was only when I read these words in a book, about the two time scales, not only did I feel vindicated, as though I had acted wisely, but all the rest came back, what my whole life could have been, and how I couldn't bear to be reduced to an orange.

The Downunders 🐌

She used to penetrate the darkest streets of the East End
with her nursing bag and once she crossed a flooded river
on horseback to bake an onion in its skin over some dying
embers: a process she described to me in recipe-like detail,
so I should remember. What I was left with was a picture:
Nan in her nurse's uniform with the red crossed ties of her
cape, two red royal orders at once, strapping the onion pith
to the outside of an ear and tying, I thought, a bandage like
a lady's motoring hat. She rode back later — here I blanched
a bit — and a long rope of pus came out of the ear, drawn by
the poultice.

They were travelling around Piccadilly Circus, going the
wrong way, and a policeman on point duty stopped them:
'You Downunders have the cheek of Old Nick!' The war was
on and in the spaces left in the rubble, little cleared parks of
normality, the office workers brought out their sandwiches
and briefcases. At the Merchant Navy Widows' Club the
widows had been told they must earn their pensions and
they hemmed sheets at long tables. Above the mantlepiece a
painted ship with apertures like an Advent calendar showed
porthole-shaped photographs of their husbands. Sometimes,
on a birthday or an anniversary, flowers in a small vase
would appear. In spite of this altar the women were
unfailingly cheerful.

This cheerfulness touched her deeply, almost made her
want to cry when the policeman said 'Downunders'. Why
she couldn't say. There was dismissal in it as well as flirtation:

the policeman had caught sight of their uniforms and waved them on as though they were wearing a flag, not the flag of the naval widows, but a recognisable cousin, with the same high colour. The nurses were piled in the back, in their crossed-over capes, laughing.

When Nan came back she brought some of it with her: the sheets that could have been shrouds, the demure picnickers. At her worst crises: when the family farm was sold and her brother came back gassed and dying from the war; when, after her fiancé was shot down, she met a truly good man but it was too late for children, she used to visualise herself in front of some grimy stairs in the East End, allowed to pass as though she was the embodiment of a lamp. Did that mean that the carload of them, rocking around Piccadilly, singing and shrieking, was some kind of incendiary bomb?

Nursing her brother, Nan wore her low bandage cap which made her eyes look owlish. He lay on his iron bedstead with its immaculate white linen and asked for books. He read *The Wild Swans at Coole* and 'Hearts with one purpose alone/Through summer and winter seem/Enchanted to a stone.' None of the war poets. Though no one would have believed him, he felt safe. It was Nan he worried about. Her profession was, thanks to him, mixed with the personal, which made it unbearable. She brought him the books he asked for and her heart quailed at the seriousness of them. Plato, *The Imitation of Christ,* writing shot through with the difficulties of a trout swimming up a weir; none of it mentioned a ship with portholes.

Nan's husband, a banker, was years older. He was a good considerate man who liked Victorian verse: volumes as dense as slab toffee, which he read while puffing a pipe. Sometimes he read a line or two to Nan, before the lamps were switched on and she took up her sewing. She filled the house with watercolours: large, unbotanic-looking shapes, just one layer of watercolour, relying on the light to animate it. Albert never said what he thought of them but I imagine he considered them imprecise.

I always wanted to be a nurse but my father forbade it. His favourite sister, my aunt Dolly, had changed before his eyes after she learnt to give bedbaths and enemas. Overnight he had no answers for her and she looked wise and mocking. It was far safer for me to be a librarian.

But I still loved hospitals, being in one for an operation. 'How long will I be in?' I tentatively asked the nurse who was prepping me. 'Ten days is about average. It depends on the surgeon.' Ten days. I counted my fingers under the sheet and checked my face in my operating gear — the operation was not until 5 p.m. — even my nail polish and foundation had been removed — at regular intervals throughout the afternoon. I knew I could bear the two drug-hazed and irritable days that led to a routine, like Nan's for her brother, that I considered safe and enchanting. It was when I began to write poems in a notebook they thought I was ready to leave.

I particularly liked the night nurse, who appeared at the bedsides just before dawn with a handful — I imagined it as a wand — of thermometers. Nan, in the year her brother was dying, slept in their father's dressing room with the door open. Her brother read to all hours and sometimes she heard him saying lines softly over to himself: '*Your arms will clasp the gathered grain/For your own good and wield the flail.*' In the distance between them she tried to send messages, arrows of love, but she knew she was outweighed by the gas. His eyes sank deeper into his head and her own eyes tried to follow as Eurydice strained to concentrate on

Orpheus. 'Don't creep up on me,' he said to her once. 'I can see you.' The night nurse, though I lay awake for her, just materialised.

Nan told me once that she had stood in a crowd of women when the soldiers disembarked. Her own fiancé was dead, she had received notification, and his last two letters arrived afterwards, full of hope and the change the war was taking. 'Be careful in the East End, Nan. I wish you would go in pairs. Grief can affect people strangely, they might attack you . . .' Women were supposed to be loose in those days and certainly some of the embraces the soldiers got almost knocked them off their feet. And the grief of those for whom there was no mate was as bitter and poleaxed as sandbags.

When she came home to New Zealand, Nan became a district nurse. The war had taught her to improvise, hence the onion. It was wrong to raise the expectations of people by appearing like a crusader. Sometimes, as she rode somewhere at night, she thought of the long years of the widows, waiting at the docks. They had formed a chorus, while those who embraced were the stars. Embraces such as she had never had, not with her honourable airman, her brother's friend, or with her brother who, even in dying, was worlds ahead. Certainly not with Albert, who was glad enough, she thought, not to embrace at all. But the Maori child with the infected ear had stopped whimpering when she bandaged his ear and the next night he had pushed his clenched fist into her palm and she had held it there, returning the pressure.

All this about Nan I am constructing. Out of what she told me and what I assumed. I have one of Albert's fusty books of verse with three ribbons for bookmarks: scarlet, gold and emerald. One of her paintings of a life-like peach and a white jug on a small table — it could be the card table we often ate off. Behind the peach there is a gap and then, as though the peach has reverberated enough — and heaven knows she worked at it and gave up oils in disgust for a time after, rubbing at it like the famous artist did with clouds with the seat of his pants — there is a small crowded window with knife-edged yachts and a sea capped with white horses. The beautiful trunk with the Spanish scarf and the photo of Nan and her dying brother I carry permanently in my head.

We met through the Art Society and quickly became friends. We played jokes on one another. I left a cauliflower on her doorstep on a day when there were no flowers in the mart buckets. She cooked too many roast vegetables and invited me down at the last moment to help eat them.

'I was really just intending to have a sandwich, Nan.'

'But you haven't had it yet?'

'I'm not sure I could eat a whole roast dinner.'

'I knew you'd be a dear and help me out.'

We sat at the card table gamely eating three roast potatoes each, a kumara and a piece of parsnip and it was barely midday. The gravy congealed in a little boat and there were yachts in the window. She drove me home in her ancient but well-preserved Morris Minor, recklessly crossing the centre line as we quoted in unison: '*The thirsty earth soaks up the rain/And drinks and gapes for drink again.*' A truck in front suddenly loosed a huge galvanised iron boiler which ran away down the road like a squealing pig.

'You'd better slow down a bit, Nan,' I said. She and the car were charmed.

You probably won't believe me but you could say I killed

Nan. If I could get a priest to listen, I'd say something like this. The preliminaries first, but I don't think I'd sit face to face, almost knee to knee, watching the priest's fingers play with the Stop/Enter button that he pressed after each absolution. If he couldn't see me, it mightn't sound so ridiculous, as though I'd been reading nothing but Mauriac for a month. 'I caused an old woman with two hip replacements to run up and down her hallway imitating a phrase, *Run like a hare*, which was the title of a poem I had written about her. She fell over the front step and died with the poem in her hand.' Not even venial, I suppose, but I gave her the idea. 'I wrote the poem' — but here I'd be interrupted because detail is not allowed, just how many apples you stole or how many sinful thoughts, how many unlawful occasions — 'sitting on a little hill in front of my child's school with his Australian terrier called Digger, who was waiting to be summoned to the classroom to perform his three tricks for Pets' Week. Sit, Lie, and Run-and-fetch a ball.' I hoped the children wouldn't notice a lack of finesse; I hoped Digger wouldn't forget everything he knew. I sat on the hillside and headed a fresh page in the manifold book: one page pink, one white with pink lines, and a carbon at the front. RUN LIKE A HARE. The rhyme and the similes just flowed; it was like a mantra. When I finished, I put 'for Nan' at the top and later I typed it out on clean paper. Digger was a triumph.

I'd be out the door and three more apple-stealers would have been shriven before I found the Prayers after Confession in the hymn book. Words that kill have no part in the preparation either, at least not in the way I understand it. You have to be a dealer in words, like the old usurers. The only words that have the power to kill are the words that lead to action. Not the words that wound, which are often over-estimated and give one a turn for wit or the quick return of weapons. But those simple pure words of praise that hide a directive. Run like a . . . jump like a . . . leap like . . . All dangerous if you are not in practice. I can still feel my pen scratching the lines on the hill, as though the hill was the climb to Robert Louis Stevenson's grave. Digger was somewhere in the bushes, snuffling over school lunch wraps. And hare: such a bold Russian steroid-reared animal. If only I had said rabbit.

So is gaiety nothing or is it everything? Perhaps this is what the policeman thought, what Nan's life showed. The car swaying under its load of Quixote-Nightingales had almost knocked him down. They were deferential, which meant they could only have been colonials. 'Don't do it again. We need you.' Unlikely as it seems, he added under his breath. But brightened in spite of himself. Then, since this was so complex, he gave the next lawbreaker a ticket.

The Girl Who Loved Mathematics &

She was tall and thin like the irreducible first number, unless you reduced it to fractions, those fey incomprehensible hieroglyphics that reminded me of freckles. I was only good at language and algebra, which was mathematics disguised, letters doing the adding for numerals or concealing themselves in a brake of brackets. We had a teacher that year who didn't like Keats but it was always considered superior to be good at maths.

As for geometry, it was, and has remained, as incomprehensible to me as some branches of modern art: Cézanne, perhaps, leading the way with his square lightly dappled boulders and trees barely held in shape, as though they stayed that way only for human perception and might otherwise fly apart into the atoms they desired to be. Any angle formed a little tent with a guy rope and the possibility of a storm: I loved Keats but wanted the world he inhabited to be flat.

But Gilberte, I'll call her that, though it's not her real name, loved mathematics with a passion. Her father was some high official who presumably dealt with estimates and figures; it was thought she inherited her talent from him. She had three brothers with no noticeable gifts at all, except riding motorbikes and drinking, and her mother was a frail doll-like woman who seemed to hang on her husband's every word.

Gilberte was good at science too and it was she who expertly made up .1 molar solutions: tapwater first and then a pipette at the end, and understood them: the rest of the class couldn't see why we needed the pipette at all. We were obviously destined to be mothers, wiping the sides of plates clean of gravy stains, while she was designed for stars and nebulae.

It was Gilberte who sensed something was wrong one day when the class was engaged in making a gas, sulphur dioxide I think it was. The teacher, who had been called away for quarter of an hour — it was safe to leave the class in Gilberte's hands and the instructions listed on the blackboard — came running up the stairs. Gilberte led us out on to the patch of grass near the Art Block where we lay on the grass for the rest of the period.

The periodic table of atoms — again I misunderstood it because my mind instantly darted into a medieval world of monastic severities and humanism, if there was such a thing in the Middle Ages. Though the atoms in their separate squares seemed severe and complete, like a chain of Carthusians, they obviously possessed the desire to join and colonise. Among these valencies and outstretched arms Gilberte moved with her own grace.

We were a motley class, except for Gilberte. It wasn't long before she outstripped her teachers, in science and maths, and there was talk of allowing her to cycle to the Boys' High School for the competition. But somehow this proposal, which might have had unforeseen benefits, was not taken up. It got so by the third term, when the teacher absented herself more and more, that Gilberte took the class. She stood on the dais and wrote the name of the experiment on the board, each step numbered. The teacher's instructions were unfailingly vague — she had been at Cambridge as a young woman, which surely promised something better than teaching us — but Gilberte wrote the method carefully, as though we were a cooking class.

Afterwards, as we had on the day of the gas, we filed out decorously and sat in the sun. (Even on the day of the gas there had been no rush: either we had not understood the seriousness or, more likely, we were remembering *The Girls of Slender Means*, which was a class book.) There was a sheltered lawn behind the old library and close to the road where none of the juniors went; though they were scornful of school, it seemed they only felt safe in its centre. Whereas we, who in a few months would escape to the outside world, had instinctively chosen a place near the road.

It was sunny and quiet on the lawn and the trees were old and gnarled with soft sparse rings of grass under them. We sat on our satchels or blazers or stretched out Roman fashion, though how the Romans ate oysters from Brittany lying on their sides was incomprehensible to me. I didn't doubt the oysters would go down but it hardly seemed comfortable.

'I expect it was so they could sprint for a feather. You know, the vomitorium,' Chrissy said.

'Easier to get up off your side,' she went on, when I looked puzzled. 'A kind of rolling start. Like a western roll.' That was the latest kind of high jump and only one of the class, Faith, had mastered it. We were not very athletic either. Still we had produced Gilberte.

'How do you know, silly?'

'I tried it one night when I was necking. At least I imagined it. I imagined I was Arria reclining with Paetus.'

'I can't imagine you and spotty Jeff committing suicide one after the other.'

'At least acne is a sign of puberty.'

'Post-puberty, I should have thought you meant. Unless Jeff is rather backward . . .'

'No, he's not backward. I should think Jeff could teach the Romans a thing or two.'

Chrissy had got up and flounced off.

Gilberte was lying on her stomach with *The Mathematical Theory of Relativity* in front of her. She gave no indication of listening. She had the kind of concentration of a blinkered horse, or the serenity, once she had pushed off, of the Lady of Shalott.

'*On either side the river lie, Long fields of barley and of rye, That clothe the wold and meet the sky,*' I said under my breath and she looked up. 'I'm sorry, I didn't mean to interrupt.'

'It's all right,' she said. 'I'm just killing time before I have to go and see the headmistress.'

'I always think those are the best lines, don't you? The beginning. Even better than the mirror, the scenery she floats through.'

'Except at that stage she hasn't seen it, it's like a tapestry.'

'I hadn't thought of that. Do you mind if I use it in an essay?'

'Go ahead. I'm not doing it anyway.'

I looked at her admiringly, because she gave me a chase in English too.

'This interview with the headmistress. If you want to talk about it . . .'

'No. It's too complicated. It's a family matter really. But thanks.'

'Are you going to the school dance?'

'I expect so.'

I was trying to get my mother to let me wear one of my dancing costumes, a Hungarian skirt with a dark navy border. She was doubtful but it seemed to me ideal for a barn dance. At any moment I might resort to the first movement of a Hungarian czardas: an hauteur so amazing a passing peasant would be frozen in his tracks or wish to be eaten by a bear.

What happened with the headmistress I never heard, because we were preoccupied with the barn dance, but I gather it was one of several interviews. The headmistress was working on Gilberte's father to let her go to university; this was common knowledge but not why Gilberte should be cloistered in the office with its imposing traffic symbols: STOP, WAIT, COME IN. I'm not even sure now if those were the messages: STOP may have meant IT'S USELESS TODAY and WAIT may have implied the headmistress would be available in ten minutes. It was a modern invention and it went with the new school assembly hall we had clambered over with the headmistress. Hadn't she said, on the one occasion she taught us, that we were the *crème de la crème* because we took Latin?

The week before the barn dance I had worked with Faith on a spider's web of string to hang over the bar. I was so preoccupied with boys, whether one would approach me in my Hungarian skirt, that the cobweb was soon over ornate and well on the way to being lace. It brought gusts of laughter from the others but I couldn't stop myself weaving.

The attitude of Gilberte's father seemed to be that boys went to university if they were so inclined and girls were homemakers and married. The fact that one of his sons had had a motorbike accident that week and the other had left school without any qualifications made no difference. If they had wished to go . . . The headmistress, whose own father had been doting, was at a loss. A meeting, an impromptu visit, perhaps at some hour designed to show her superiority — this would be a little unfair on Gilberte's mother, who might be caught peeling potatoes.

'Is there a family history of illness, any debility?' the headmistress had asked as she chainsmoked. 'Anything that might make an academic career a necessary protection?'

But Gilberte couldn't think of anything. She sat, not unlike her mother, with her hands in her lap and her fair head downcast; she was not even thinking of the dance, since she was, besides the brightest girl in class, also the tallest. Statistics were against there being many tall boys.

'You *would* like to go, Gilberte?' the headmistress asked. 'To spend the next three years studying maths or science.'

'Pure mathematics. I should like to study pure mathematics.'

'I took Greats,' the headmistress said, fitting a fresh cigarette into her ebony holder. Girls had been expelled from the bushes for less. 'Punting — of course there are no punts in Auckland, or wherever it is you would be going. We must find the best professor. Perhaps I could write to him. It is the final school that produces the best days of your life.'

When Gilberte still said nothing and continued to look at her hands, the headmistress said, 'I'll write to your father and ask him to call one evening.'

Adamantine, the headmistress thought. That is what Gilberte's father is. But how to deal with him? His love of figures; the genetic brilliance that had skipped his sons and alighted on the head of his daughter; the scandal of a talent gone to waste. She foresaw it would be useless to pick the wrong option; it was like a lucky dip. She must have a word to the science mistress about genetics. There was a rumour that one of the sons was up before the magistrate.

I managed to get my Hungarian skirt out of my mother and there were enough short boys for partners so I disowned the cobweb. A large black spider was fastened in the centre of it. There was one very tall boy for Gilberte and between dances we sat out on hay bales beneath the parallel bars. There was a line between her brows and she seemed, who was adept at every combination of atoms, to be concentrating on the m.c.

The next day Gilberte was called out of the double period of science and when she returned, her eyes were red. The barn dance had given me an insight into valencies: the inept and hesitant way male and female hands joined — some of the boys should wear gloves, Chrissy had complained, and others held your hand like a wet fish — made me think that elements too knew an initial hesitancy which was only overcome at the last moment, possibly by an external director. But the boldest atoms seized their partners round the waist and swept them into an embrace.

We were sitting under the library trees again, discussing boys. There was Beatrice, who was knitting a complex sweater for her boyfriend. They were so committed they seemed almost married: her tall hairy-legged boyfriend need only don long trousers, sweater and a pipe and I saw them settled for life. At the end-of-year senior ball the headmistress and senior mistresses sat on the stage in rows, wearing their academic gowns. 'A last warning of what we have missed,' Chrissy would say.

Whether the headmistress wore her gown at her interviews with Gilberte's father I am not sure. There were several interviews. Sometimes Gilberte's mother came too, though she probably added very little. Gilberte herself, apart from stating her love of mathematics, probably said little as well; perhaps the headmistress was hoping for an impassioned plea, a little Marie Curie. But the father remained adamant. Gilberte's gifts were of course a compliment to his own bent for figures, a gift which nature had not bestowed on his sons. But he believed it should be regarded as nothing more than a fluke. Here the headmistress must have resisted the desire to press the STOP button under her desk or to catapult him from his chair, a device that was not yet installed. 'She has the heart and soul of her mother,' she thought. The father's success was beginning to seem very conditional.

'Gilberte,' she counselled the quiet lank girl, giving up part of her lunch hour and asking that coffee be brought, an unheard-of compliment. She felt as if she might be fighting for the life of a future Nobel Prize winner. In that case a special board would have to be made to go alongside the Dux and Excellence in Work and Sport. 'You must fight, with whatever strength you've got. You are not strong and the sheltered life of the academy, the introduction to young men who would understand your merit, the attentions of professors, after the first anonymous year in a class of 200 pure mathematicians, would give you the security I fear you need. Your father's idea of security is quite a different thing.'

'Do you see me married to an academic?' Gilberte asked, casting an eye towards Beatrice's knitting and drawing her long legs further under her so she was inside the valency of shade cast by the tree.

'The headmistress seems to think I should. Be grateful, I mean.'

'You haven't had much to compare one with. Have you ever met a professor?'

'I suppose Dr Petrovsky could be an example.'

'I certainly don't fancy Dr Petrovsky. We're all terrified of him.'

'Of course he is no longer engaged in research, which may be the cause of his bad temper. And the fact that we don't do our homework. You do, of course.'

'I think she means someone quiet and dreamy who will smile when I mention the pleasure of numbers. Someone in the same field to talk projective geometry with in the evenings. Do you think that is likely?'

'I think she wants to see you protected. Like a rare white albino. Or the class unicorn. Then when you are justly famous she can put your name on a board outside her office, like a stuffed moose.'

She smiled suddenly and I couldn't tell whether it was maths she was thinking of, or the moose.

The end of the year was nearly on us. Our final exams were over and a few lazy weeks were left. One by one we had trooped to visit the careers advisor and those who were not obviously nurses or teachers, a minority, were advised to supplement their skills with typing classes. I sat in the back of a fourth form class and mastered the keyboard in the last term. Chrissy was going to be a dentist's technician; Beatrice put down her knitting long enough to enrol for physiotherapy. 'I suppose you'll treat your patients like wool strung on needles,' Chrissy had called out and for a moment I had a vision of a Heath Robinson contraption and legs in white plaster.

One day I walked with Gilberte around the field above the boarding school. A few sixth formers, those who had not been accredited, were walking about, talking to themselves with books tightly closed, or lying face down on the bleached grass.

'Romantic, isn't it?' I said. 'Though not to the swots.'

'I suppose they've come up here to escape distractions. Those who have passed can be rather cruel.'

'A life passed in study and learned pursuits. Rather nun-like in a way. I suppose they are not allowed to go to dances either.'

'At least if they pass they will have done it on their own merits. This is what the headmistress says.'

I remembered a time I had heard her console a weeping girl who had failed some exam with a terse 'It's only a year in your life, child. What a fuss over a year!'

One lunch hour I escaped before the bell and walked to a French pastry shop at the corner and filled my capacious black umbrella with meat pies, which we ate under the trees. Why in the years at school had I not been more daring, I wondered. I was going to be a librarian and take some extra-mural units. In a few weeks I would be overdressed and sitting surrounded by pots of paste, invisible tape and date slips, with a pile of dog-eared books beside me as I learned to 'mend'.

I would be at the prizegiving but not the last assembly. One more singing of brutal 'Gaudeamus', so much less charitable than Shakespeare's seven stages of man, though Shakespeare tended to overdo senility. A speech about achievement and the headmistress in a stunning sheath over which her cap and gown presided like a presentiment of the mighty wing. She was rumoured to be highly nervous because of the presence of the board of governors.

But Gilberte was not at the prizegiving. Not there to receive her dux's ring and to go up last on the stage where the lower ranks had gone in threes and twos. There was a rumour that her father had taken her away from school and she was going to be his secretary. The headmistress made an apology which I thought was tinged with anger; and her address was on the wastage of women's abilities, a wastage she had given her life to prevent, though at the same time she set a reassuring example of smoking and drinking gin and tonic. I think that was why we respected her. I've never forgotten the day it was my turn in her office and I found her sitting in her exclusive underwear behind the desk, lighting one cigarette from the stub of another. 'Don't stare, girl,' she said. 'Can't you see I've spilt my coffee? We can carry on as though nothing has happened.'

'What is *your* side of the story?' she used to say to a girl sent out to stand in the corridor and eventually led to her office, like a fly to a spider. But Gilberte had gone and Gilberte's father had lain still and escaped by his superior masculine strength. Her speech had an edge that evening, a pace like Keats composing in top form.

Beatrice told me what had happened. She was a boarder and she had witnessed more of the evening meetings than the rest of us who were day girls. It seems the headmistress, though it was a little hard to tell from a distance, had extended her hand in what seemed a gesture of goodwill and further meetings and then at the last moment her hand had struck Gilberte's father's face.

'It sounds like science fiction,' I said disbelievingly, when we were sitting in a coffee bar during my lunch hour. 'Are you sure you were not mistaken?'

But she swore it was true. 'It was like that Ngaio Marsh story where the sky turns black when you've killed a rabbit.'

But I preferred to think that the headmistress had been seized by Gilberte's love of mathematics and her hand had risen in the shape of the first numeral.

All I know of Gilberte is what Chrissy told me. She married the first man she met at a dance, had five children, and ran a fish and chip shop. At least she could add the numbers in her head.

A World Elsewhere ❧

On the third day, when Clare turned the now-familiar lock on her door on the twelfth floor, she saw the author named LeRoi doing the same three doors along. His eye caught hers and he nodded with a faint trace of surprise, as though up until then he hadn't realised they were on the same floor.

Clare imagined a moue of regret and then told herself she was being foolish. LeRoi was married and she had stood alongside him at the checkout in the souvenir shop at Niagara Falls while he purchased two sweatshirts with CANADA on them for his children. Though he had bought all the women writers a single rose with their names on and a message: *Clare, from LeRoi, with a kiss,* he had hardly spoken to them during the festival, except those he was seated next to at dinner.

Clare had had trouble with the door to her suite after the first unlocking and a bellboy had to be summoned to explain that in Canada keys turn to the left. And the faucets in the bathroom, over the basin and over the bath, had required a good five minutes' wrenching and pushing until she mastered them. A note addressed to all the authors, on the dressing table, mentioned an author of a previous year who had failed for three days to have a bath. Another, determined to attend every session, had been visited with misfortune, broken a leg and had a publisher's option cancelled.

When she arrived, Clare had been too excited to sleep and had gone straight down to the foyer where a famous author was being honoured and a buffet was in its closing stages. The famous author could be seen only in the distance, surrounded by television cameras and speaking softly and deliberately. Instead Clare found herself in a glassed-in patio with a group of authors, some of them, who had arrived only hours or a day before herself, equally culture-shocked. It seemed the buffet *was* dinner and there was only an hour before the readings. It was miraculous how everything fell into a pattern. Before she went up to her suite for her coat, Clare had learned not only about breakfast and how to get to the city but the location of a discreet clothesline above the bath.

The theatre where the readings were held was two blocks from the hotel. It was a huge complex with fountains and escalators and glass elevators. Once it had been a ferry terminus and on three sides were berthed the launches that made excursions on the lake. The theatre, on the top floor, was the size of a small opera house.

Clare had noticed Lawrence watching her during the second bracket of readings after the interval, when she had left the authors' box (plush red boxes, one on each side of the stage, from which the authors could wave across to each other and make gestures of helplessness if it was their turn to read) because she felt the need to cough. The foyer with its floor-length mirrors and displays of books for autographing was deserted now, except for the bar staff cleaning up after the rush. Clare bought another Canada Dry and walked about, not, she thought, unlike Miss Bingley or Elizabeth Bennet in front of Mr Darcy. Not that she imagined Lawrence, whose name she did not know then, as Mr Darcy — he was simply a dark rather attentive shape — rather it was so many mirrors catching all aspects of her promenade that made her feel self-conscious as though, like Elizabeth Bennet, she had forgotten how to walk.

During the interval Clare sat next to a woman who told her she was aiming to write a journal. Clare, who had written two journals and a third abandoned one, advised her to divide it into seasons so she wouldn't feel obliged to write every day. She didn't caution that seasons were also inflexible and it was hard to escape introspection, even if you anticipated it by beginning on your birthday. After they had talked, the woman insisted on buying one of Clare's own books for Clare to sign. She wrote in it *'To Esmé, with warm wishes for your journal'* and for a moment they clutched hands.

The next evening Lawrence was on duty again and he came up to her in the crush. 'A man's been looking for you for the last three nights. I think he wants to take a photo or arrange an interview. I told him I'd look out for you.'

'How am I going to recognise him?'

'I'll describe him to you. He's quite old' — Clare's heart sank, ever since she arrived in Canada she had been expecting some exciting encounter — 'with small veins on his cheeks. Middle height. He said he'll be standing over by the posters. If I see him tonight, I'll introduce you.'

Each evening after the last reading the Hospitality Suite was open for a nightcap. The bath was filled with ice and out of it rose titanic quantities of alcohol, floating like life buoys. As fast as one bottle was rescued another sank. On the final night, when the two most famous authors had read, and two other authors were presented with word processors, there were cases of champagne.

Clare and Lawrence were sitting on one of the black leather sofas and drinking far too much. Clare leaned back against the padding and her glass was refilled without her being aware she held it out. Her room was on the same floor; she could excuse herself and powder her nose and slip back in again, without anyone noticing.

Lawrence was talking to her rather intimately, it seemed, though she did not catch every word. There was such a hum in the room. It was their last assault on the bathtub. Every now and again someone would let out a whoop for a shared opinion or a common insight or simply because most of them were leaving in the morning. Night after night Clare had drunk Canada Dry, wanting to preserve her senses. The champagne was like opening a lot of presents.

'Any woman can give a man satisfaction. It's something women don't realise.'

'Do you mean, at night all cats are grey?' Clare wasn't sure she had the quote right. Is this what men really think, she wondered. In which case Lawrence's attention was hardly a compliment. In the dimly lit room, sinking into the leather, Clare did suddenly feel grey. To compensate she leaned forward and tried to look at Lawrence directly.

He was very handsome in an unmarked way. Hair very dark, skin very unblemished and uniformly pale. He had certainly never had acne. His lashes were unfairly long and the eyes grey. Perhaps there was a little too much space between the nose and the mouth, and the mouth itself lacked definition, as if it hadn't been used overmuch.

When they first sat down they had talked about Lawrence's problems of being a part-time opera singer with a fiancée and a flat and certain material expectations. The Oxford University Press representatives who had taken Clare to lunch on the day of her reading, a day she felt so ill she thought she might be sick in an underground car park, had told her that CANADA meant NOTHING or something like it. She had recovered and they had ordered something sensible for her in a restaurant called Tall Poppies, which they had thought might appeal. She had never felt less like a tall poppy. On the way back to the hotel the prettiest among the girls had had her car impounded in the grounds of a Catholic church but Clare had managed to hold the chain aloft and the car had driven under it, like someone escaping confession.

'Why not take a chance for a few years?' Clare asked. 'Would your fiancée mind? You might have a good career and be wealthy before you know it.'

In her own country — 'I never realised until my last visit New Zealand was so poor,' the organiser had said to her; it was on the day of LeRoi's roses and luckily no one had been standing very close — the really aristocratic people often seemed shabby. One house that belonged to the brother of a deceased poet had sofas with stuffing protruding on the verandahs and shoes left in the closets grew mould. But really important things: a cherry orchard growing to the riverbank, a black Steinway grand with a voluptuous oil of a nude behind it, and blue Italian glass plates for scrambled egg, were more than a screen. Did an opera singer need chandeliers?

Clare sensed Lawrence was not really listening, or thinking of something else. His fiancée dogged him, as though sleeping together meant they could never be apart in daylight. 'We missed each other once by waiting on the wrong corner. We were only a few yards apart. It made her frantic.'

And then he had said something about all women being the same or equally useful. Equally possible for a man to use, and if the rare one was too ugly, Clare imagined, a paper bag over the head would do the trick. He was leaning towards her in such a confiding way that she could not get up even if she tried. And straight after he said something about how intelligent she was and how good it was talking to her.

The man who had been looking for her had not seemed so old after all. Although Clare looked hard at his cheeks, she couldn't see any incipient veins. His eyes were pouchy and slightly tired-looking but his coming back, though surely she was not the sole reason, was a compliment. He was an editor, he explained. He'd just like a couple of photos for his column. He took one of her standing against the wall with posters and another 'just looking up under your chin'. We understand each other, she thought, he's thinking of the possibility of double chins. She thanked him warmly, aware that Lawrence was watching.

All the authors had got wet at Niagara Falls although they were in long black raincoats. 'Like a crowd of Jesuits,' someone said. Clare's makeup had run and it had ruined the elegant lunch at Niagara-on-the-Lake where she had sat with a cameraman and a film producer. The mist had descended on them in a downpour and she had held her tape recorder out to catch the roar. On the morning of the Oxford lunch her throat was aching and she had gone in search of the hotel doctor who, she was sure, regarded her as a hypochondriac. 'You have conference-itis,' he told her. 'Try not to talk until you have to.' She had read without worrying about expression at all, just whether her new deep voice would hold out.

'Would you excuse me for a moment while I go and get another throat lozenge?'

'Certainly,' Lawrence said.

'I'll be right back. Don't go away.' Just the same, she could see he was a little rebuffed.

Her room was just a horseshoe loop away. She twisted the key to the left and poured herself a long glass of water — from Lake Ontario? — and looked at twelve reflections of her face in the strip mirror with its makeup lights sufficient to reveal the tiniest veins or the shadow where a chin might come. The bed with its russet cover was as hard as a football field and she had slept each night with a sleeping pill. But Lawrence, if his theory was right, might have preferred a hard bed. 'Would you excuse me while I get a throat lozenge' was not exactly a turn on. She had no intention of taking another throat lozenge ever. She had been inundated: some of the authors had even sent samples for her to try from box to box. An American friend had scoured the chemists near the hotel for Fisherman's Friend.

When she got back to the party, Lawrence was chatting up another woman who was leaning on every word. Clare went into the tiny kitchen, where one of the staff was cutting lemons, and fished for a club soda in the bath. The ice was mushy and thawing. 'A New Zealander. I must meet a genuine nuclear-free New Zealander before I go,' someone called and she was led over, like a breed of rare dog, and a French Canadian, disloyally urging her to 'get rid of the French too', shook her hand with fervour. He was tall and handsome but she resented being a diplomat. 'We've got a New Zealander in our office,' a Canadian editor's wife had told her. 'I hate her. When I heard your accent I thought, Oh no, not another one.'

Some of the stragglers were talking of going dancing and Lawrence looked as though he might be interested. He was standing a little to one side and Clare went up to him and said, 'There you are.'

'Opera gives you a taste for late nights. And early mornings. Did I tell you that?'

'No, but I guessed.'

'You won't come dancing?'

'I think not.'

'So I won't see you again?'

'You must have faith in opera. Perhaps you will.'

'If you write your address, I'll send you a card.'

Clare wrote it on the back of a programme and in spite of the glass of water her handwriting was almost illegible.

'What sort of postcard shall I send you?'

'Something to remind me of Toronto. What about the bank with the bronze cattle outside it. The raw material and the end result?'

'I won't forget.'

She could call up room service and have a giant cheeseburger sent up, with chips on the side and Coke, but she had already done that, after the reading. She had propped herself on the incredibly firm bed and watched Joan Rivers and then a replay of the Boston Red Sox. It would be good for Lawrence to go in search of the bank with the cattle, which he admitted he had never seen. The faces of the cattle were so jowly and heavy, they definitely required a bag over their heads. But perhaps Lawrence was right too: they had produced such a long straight shining shaft of wealth.

Librarians &

I feel I want to set them down as cameos. Libraries are routines, like life. The miracle is librarians have life at all.

1

I met Laila at Library School in the days when part of it, a standing joke, like the complexities of the Union Catalogue, was housed above a Chinese laundry. Laila was standing in the street below Parliament and carrying a large hatbox secured with a dull green ribbon. We became friends when we received our first assignment: an exercise in compiling a bibliography of a literary figure, to be done in pairs. Working together gave us odd hours of pleasure: going to films seldom seen at provincial cinemas, having extravagant lunches and meagre suppers, trying on hats in a department store. A man approached us one day in James Smith's and asked first Laila and then me for a date. We fled giggling and shared a banana split. All around us serious librarians were having breakdowns and being undone by *See also* entries. It was a time of great purity in librarianship. Every book must have an author, even if it took a microscope to find: it was like shelving home a moral responsibility. Imprint dates could not be evaded and no one could be known as Bill or Joe or Sam. The reference librarian, an eccentric Pole, locked the whole class in the reference section until we had answered a question. Mine was about a film star: I found the answer in *Film Guide*. Laila's too was simple: the date of a piece of music, locatable in *Groves*. Some of the class were kept in until nightfall. After a week Laila confessed she was in love with a farmer who came from a family of bachelors. Some weekends she went home to watch him ploughing. I've no idea if she got him to succumb eventually. Or if she ever wore the hat.

2

Beverly's father had knocked all the lights in a street off when he was driving a double-decker bus in London and her brother was a gambler who, when he died, was buried with a pack of cards. Beverly herself was a fluttery creature, treating each request for information or registration as a panic. She ran with wild arm motions and her hands flapped like wings. We sat in the workroom pushing long needles that might have been vicious in other hands through stacks of pink, green, yellow and beige issue cards. Where there were gaps a book was overdue. We worked with a bossy assistant called Renata, who felt she had to call in during her annual holidays to check what we were doing. I was not yet trusted with the cards or needles, only with writing the addresses on the front of the overdue notices and adding an 's' to 'book' when there was more than one outstanding. The card was headed coyly DID YOU FORGET? in order not to deter the timid. Beverly was timid and she meant to be welcoming but her little high-pitched cries and rapid speech sometimes made her almost unintelligible. When I was considered experienced enough to work at night, I worked Wednesdays with her: one of the best and quietest nights, since few people knew the library was open then, and, already partly a librarian, I didn't think they should be told. Beverly had a curious habit when it came to counting the day's takings:

she spread the small, but to her baffling, amounts for fines, reserves, replacement cards, library bags on the floor and sat in the middle on her heels. 'This way the piles don't get mixed,' she used to say. We wrapped the coins in twists of paper, torn with a ruler. She lunched at a dismal little café smelling of disinfectant and one day she met her husband there: a gentle man thirty years older than her, with a grownup family.

3

The old brick Carnegie Library, with the Carnegie seal in stone over the entrance and its dove-grey steps, was controlled by Miss Rosevear. She was a legend like an earlier first assistant, Miss Free. Miss Free and Rental, but I doubted the library had the free and rental system then: no book resembling a rental would have been admitted, though in the Children's section, governed by an equally fierce lady, I did once manage to get my hands on a new Enid Blyton Secret Seven adventure and hold on, though the vanquished child dealt me a kick in the shins. Why were these early librarians so fierce? Miss Rosevear, in a display taken from the library archives to celebrate twenty-five years of the new library, which rose out of the old Carnegie optimism once it had been reduced to rubble, is pictured saying she had to sacrifice her social life to her job. She also says she hardly had time to read but could match people to books by remembering what someone liked and passing it on to a similar borrower. Which librarian, detecting someone has exhausted the Zane Greys and Louis L'Amours, has not done the same by leading, or rather lassooing, the unhorsed one toward Gerald Durrell? But to make a virtue of it? Miss Rosevear has a very tight mouth and her glasses are the no-nonsense sort worn by Elton John. But the worst thing I know about Miss Rosevear, though I can imagine her loneliness and sympathise with it — what dragon's heart fails to have juice inside? — is her behaviour over dusting. At 8.30 a.m. we still take our wooden-handled lambswool dusters out of the store cupboard where they are stowed like so many sticks of candy floss and advance towards a section of the shelves, a different section every month. There we proceed to tickle the bald foreheads of Dickens and Dostoevsky, and flick the remaining fifth of bare shelf where the new authors, yet to be born, will come. When this space is wide enough, we set a book in the spotlight, face to the borrower, and give it a special spring clean. But Miss Rosevear had her staff bang the heavy novels of those days — the Dostoevsky and Dickens — together and if the banging stopped or died in some section of the shelves — she must have had musical ears — she pounced.

4

Mary-Jane, of all the librarians I worked with, was the most perfect. Besides being beautiful, fine-boned but strong, with slender ankles, shiny shoes and well-manicured hands, she was as patient as Pamela, as calm as a mill pond and as equable as a highly trained diplomat. Her writing on memos, reserves, interloans, registrations, could be read at a glance and she rang the reserves in a deep mellifluous voice with a hint of intimacy that belied her straightness. Perhaps her strides were a little long or she pushed a trolley with an enthusiastic masculine strength but that would be like criticising one of the daughters of Leah. I wanted to know if her straightness of character, the straightness of the legendary George Washington, could last a lifetime. Yet I think she was curiously unaffected by books: I doubt she ever read anything dangerous or frivolous. She would have been equally at home with gold bars. I was slightly pained, I confess, when my fiancé, late one Friday night when we were pushing up, asked Mary-Jane to remove her shoes so he could see her feet, and declared them perfect, as he had suspected. Predictably she fell in love with a young man of good family who was unfortunately promised to a girl with an impediment. The young man was a great triathlete and Mary-Jane began to take out books on diets. His family owned a nightclub and Mary-Jane and her parents often went there for lunch. Mary-Jane returned from these lunches faintly flushed and pushed trolleys with even greater enthusiasm. She was defeated in the end by her straightness: her lovely strength and nobility — for I'm sure she deserved those words — couldn't or wouldn't resort to any subterfuge but waiting, available in the wings, whatever the wings of the athletic field are called. The mother of the promised girl intervened and the marriage was announced. I like to think of Mary-Jane considering darker, disappointing books for a time. It was a short hiatus, however, then Mary-Jane herself was claimed by an admirer who had been watching her from the wings.

5

Sabina wore a red and emerald diamond-patterned mini dress and was summoned into the Librarian's office and rebuked for peeptoe shoes and red toenails. Hairpins fell out of my French roll, which I was wearing in imitation of Catherine Deneuve, and a borrower had complained. I identified with Sabina, who loved books and collected only hardbacks. She gave me a list of American novelists I had never heard of, works about factory girls and small Midwest farms, Faulkner descendants. We dropped *By Love Possessed* on the floor and it opened at a page with the phrase 'central hairy diadem' whose incongruity still impresses. At Library School they had told us this was the way to find the dirty bits. And we tried to devise a system to track down a borrower who cut sections out with almost surgical precision. For all her love of books Sabina was displaced. She wanted systems that worked, that were the basis of knowledge, the way an underground car park is located below a great hotel. But there was something in libraries that glorified systems and slowed them down, tortoise-like. And she could not tolerate the idiocy of borrowers who tried to track down 'a book with a yellow cover'. She expected books to answer questions. We worked on a Discard List in the stackroom together, she reading the titles to me as I wrote them on cards. *Aeschylus, 525-456 B.C. Tragedies. Trans. by G. M. Cookson. Everyman, 1955.* 'Poor Aeschylus,' she said. 'This must be like crossing the Styx for him.' When the replies came in, we stamped them in order of arrival and then overthrew the system to allot at least some of their requests to small deserving libraries. We sent volume 1 of Proust — the likeliest to go missing — to a tiny one-horse town. One day Sabina came to work in a more outrageous outfit than usual, got into a frightful argument with a borrower, and stormed out. She became a missionary, a computer programmer, and finally a socialite in the mould of Elsa Maxwell.

6

Daniel grew up in a family of girls and was the star of his year's crop of trainees. He was like a male ballet dancer, singled out for his sex, because he leaps higher or faces the scorn of more callow youths. He got around this by adopting the style of Groucho Marx. He dressed in very tight black drainpipe trousers, gaudy American sneakers which made his long feet look enormous and checked shirts whose tails hung loose. He kept up a constant flirtation with all the lower orders and those higher up, once he discovered their weak spots. The older librarians were vulnerable to his gangly, half-nourished charm and at a staff function it was discovered he could play the trumpet. For Thursday morning reference sessions, when the staff took turns to prepare queries based on reference books, his were the curliest.

'What social function is served by milk money?' took half an hour to locate in *A Dictionary of Anthropological Terms.* When I finally found it, 'a small gift to the bride's mother by the son-in-law', I thought how well it suited Daniel and that for all his mobile face, he was really as secretive in his black stovepipes as an African mask. He was a clone, separated by twenty-five years — I had left work to raise a family, come back to relieve while someone was at Library School, divorced, stayed — of my first Librarian: a home-birther, vague but cunning inside it, always walking about on crepe soles and coming up behind you, typing reports with two fingers, illustrating — and how he illustrated this — the virtue of flirting with revolutionary ideas. 'Know, when you introduce an idea, when to stop and act indifferent,' he used to say, knowing his staff were uncomprehending and therefore safe. 'Then introduce it again, carelessly as a lost memorandum, in three months' time. Praise those who accept it and perceive its virtues.' Perhaps he had left this message in the walls or behind where the duster reached — Daniel dusted too, with proper Groucho Marx style, wielding it like a baton — and it was being absorbed, as I still naively

believed a book was, or as I knew myself to have been, by
Elizabeth Bennet, Emma Bovary, Colette's red-haired Annie
with the revolver.

7

In the late afternoon, when the franking machine being
worked by the secretary had the same consoling sound as
milk bottles being put out or the clock being wound, only
Mercedes had any sparkle left. She sailed in each morning
like the first blessèd galleon, carrying all the library's hopes,
soon to be defeated, of an unusually stimulating day, a
borrower requiring extraordinary tact, a reference query of
stupefying difficulty that must be despatched with speed. It
was nothing for her, on the Information desk, with its
returns module: a kind of covered-wagons-at-siege-by-
Indians blockade of trolleys, VCR terminal and wand which
passed over each accession number and beeped a message,
to answer three questions at once and flirt with a fourth.
She shone through sleeplessness, migraines that would have
felled others, domestic upheavals, the death of parents. As
Children's Librarian she had donned witch's nose and
broomstick and flown into the centre of adoring children.
She flew everywhere, circulating, the titular Head of
Circulation. And we, because she invited it, like a field of
electricity left in a comb, tumbled after her, though leaving
her as the sole galleon. Her collisions with the City Librarian
were legion but quickly over and I thought her promotion
had robbed her of a little daring: the enticements of being
management and standing together in front of a shelf
labelled: *To be looked at by CL or HofC*. Occasionally someone
had to be reprimanded and would be led upstairs to the
staffroom — not at morning or afternoon tea, naturally —

and a fast, bitter (some of the juniors were not as impressed by authority as they might have been and, besides, shelving, instead of subduing them, had fomented a kind of rebellion) exchange took place. Afterwards the culprit was always included in the gaiety. To watch someone hurl themself against a daily grind with all their resources of courage and vitality is a moving sight but I am not sure the library is the best place for it. A struggle between a saint and her God is at least clear cut: scorpions and desires of the flesh. I often wished there was some decoration I could bestow on Mercy, as once, when we were both less senior, I stuck a silver star on the centre of her clear narrow forehead and congratulated her on being a Sneetch.

8

Six steel shelves of new books fell on Louella when she was crouched on the floor, barefoot, among boxes of orders and invoices. Luckily her head was half way under the desk, which cracked in two under the weight. Pinioned, she uttered faint cries — it was a Wednesday night with only two seniors and the student shelvers. A trailing vine fell with the books and lay across her, like a Burne-Jones. Such things were always happening to Louella: it was impossible for her to cross through Woolworths, on her way to one of the two local bookshops the library patronised, without getting her clothing streaked by a child in a pushchair with an ice-cream. After the collapse of the shelves some of the taller books were removed and the trailing vine was cut in segments and distributed: I have a piece of it growing, infinitesimally slowly, on a side-table. Louella had the most wonderful excuses for not coming in to work: time reacted to her as it did to the Mad Hatter; the electricity in her body sent any watch crazy. She had freakish illnesses that perpetually puzzled her doctor: allergies, fainting spells. She was playful too, with the playfulness of the Mafia. A bully with a kind heart once you bested her and an amazing vulnerability. Some days I couldn't, though I was supposed to be a writer, come anywhere near her for wisecracks: she could catch your nerves and throw you off balance. Other times she was confiding, like the time she told me she was learning to see relationships — she was in a stormy one with a very unlikely man — as finite and precious. We discussed orders together and she accused me of ordering the same book six times: I stole the *Bookseller* from her and she chased me with a ruler. She flirted with males and females indiscriminately and in summer she sometimes wore plunging necklines to cheer the borrowers.

'Louella, I can see your cleavage.'

'I was hoping you would. Now you've seen it, what do you think of it?'

She was a bit like St Peter: all wobble. Just the same, when I think of such an amorphous place having a heart, I think of Louella.

9

We are sitting on the stairs at a staff meeting. We used to meet in the workroom, where the cunning grabbed the typists' chairs. Now we sit on the newly carpeted blue stairs as though we are in a lecture theatre. Mishaps with routines, a complaint from a borrower over a too-casual response — no one is owning up to this, we are all looking blank. Then there is a shift in tone — they are quite well constructed, these meetings, like a catalogue card — and someone is congratulated on becoming engaged or passing the first part of the Library Certificate. There are reference books at the end that the typists and receptionist do not stay for but before that someone suggests the library bus should be entered in the Christmas parade. I groan inwardly, since it soon becomes clear the bus must be preceded by librarians dressed as characters out of books. The Community Services Librarian, whose job it is to entice borrowers into the library, a kind of raw material, like patients in doctors' waiting rooms, is already looking alert and taking notes. Mercy threatens to kick the proposer of the idea in the shins but I can see she is excited too. Louella is volunteering to go as a witch. Consorts are included and the student shelvers. A few days later giant facsimile books are being assembled with cardboard covers, boxed-in sides, and dust-jackets enlarged on the Xerox. *The Detective Omnibus*, reads one, to accompany a detective in a false nose, a deerstalker and a wig with silver thread. I've tried to find a nun's costume but when the theatre company have their nuns on hire, I haven't the nerve to ring the convent. Instead I have hired, from a visiting oilman's wife, a black throat-to-ankle robe with a hood. It's in a shiny material and is hung with plastic bats and at the belt are four very realistic white mice complete with whiskers. My black gloves, which will close over *The Book of Do-It-Yourself Spells*, have spider rings. Some heavy pancake, purple eyeshadow and brown lipstick will, I hope, render me invisible.

10

So here we all are: librarians in front of the library bus, which is being driven by the Children's Librarian in a chauffeur's outfit. We have balloons at our wrists and our hands hold our books face outwards, illustrating a wonderful variety, if these potential subscribers, three deep, can be got off the streets. Mercy is touting for custom, dressed as a jester, and some small children look slightly alarmed. How shocked Miss Rosevear would be, I think, unless of course she was banging a drum. Mary-Jane would be smiling with her head slightly raised, perhaps seeing in these hollow books the purpose of libraries for the first time; Beverly would be as confused as ever; and Laila would be wearing her ever-hopeful hat. Sabina I really miss, as though she, of all of us, has escaped with the contents of books. Daniel is there of course as Groucho Marx. Last but not least there is the Saint Bernard that belongs to Kathryn, who is dressed as a monk. After we've parked the bus in the centre of the playing field, I get a big green plastic watering can out of the bus and go to find it some water. The cricket pavilion is closed but behind it I find a small stream. I crouch down beside it and hold the watering can under. A man comes around the corner, sees me and almost faints. I see myself too: a cowled figure with a chalk-white face, hung with sacrificial bats and mice. For a moment I am as rich as a book, I am the inside of myself.

In Memory of Bee 🐝

The house was so remarkably clean when we got there, even though it was her wedding day, I cornered Bee and asked her how she had done it.

'A little at a time,' she replied, looking wise. 'A tiny corner one day, another the next and so on.'

It had been such a variable house when her husband had lived there on his own, except that Rupert was never alone, he was always with or between women. The bedroom must have had as many layers of paint as there were in the paintbox: I could remember a dark midnight blue, the brown that was once called 'nigger' and a lemon that went with the early morning light.

Today it was closed and there were just the two small suitcases on the bed and Bee's makeup case, almost the size of the suitcase. She was comedienne mainly, but she had played in Pinter at which she was surprisingly effective; the long pauses gave full use to her eyes.

The kitchen though had always stayed a bright yellow, a sharp blinding citrus taste. Several of the ladies had threatened to change it but none had. Perhaps because it was Rupert's choice. I remember the kitchen because later in the day when some of the guests thought of washing glasses, no one could find the sink plug.

Beyond the kitchen, which bisected the house like a long bright gallery, was a large open room with a couple of smaller rooms leading off. And beyond the large room a full floor-to-ceiling sweep of (very clean) window, uncurtained, filled with the colours of bush and sky and estuary. The other verandah, where one entered, was made of slats in some natural wood and was overhung with baskets and baskets of trailing pink begonias.

Rupert's women were all vibrant: one had been a television frontperson, another a lieder singer, one (Pippin & Philippa) designed children's clothes; only one had been a night nurse. There had been two wives, or was it three? — I was never sure whether Bee was three or four — but they seemed part of the procession and hardly more distinguishable than the mistresses. Sometimes the mistresses turned into wives, which was usually a fatal mistake, since it's an almost impossible transition.

Rupert himself was a photographer, free-lance. He was an astute businessman, just a few paces behind Lord Lichfield. Bee corresponded in his life, I thought, with Lord Lichfield's own bride. He certainly looked exceedingly moved at the wedding.

I remember it as a beautiful day. The citrus kitchen glowed beatifically, the fresh panes struck non-smear glints off the parquet floor, which was so clean one could have eaten off it; even the begonias looked as though they had been polished. A big tray of champagne glasses with brandy and sugar cubes dissolving in it stood ready for a lethal toast.

The ceremony was held in a courtyard shaded by a banana palm. This banana palm was a curiosity: its fruit, of which there were fewer than five each year, were practically straight; it may have had something to do with the city's being only semi-tropical, from December to the end of February. This was late October and I remember feeling grateful.

I watched Bee's face as the ring was slipped on her finger and thought I had never seen her so undone on stage. Rupert beside her seemed a model of solicitude; he bent slightly forward as though admiring her third digit, looking for broken bones. There was a tiny pause as her knuckle was slightly swollen, a tiny hiatus, and then the audience broke into spontaneous applause.

After that Bee's housekeeping was methodically undone and impressions come to me only in cameos. A group sitting on the bed in the guest room with a Turkish love pillow, one of the gifts, between them. (They were telling dirty jokes.) The kitchen blazing and dividing the guests into light and shade. Someone asking the officiating minister if he was unfrocked — there was a rumour circulating. Someone in a German helmet clutching a stem of agapanthus and saying that Rupert was always at his most hypocritical when he was looking most sincere. Bee's frock becoming a bit bedraggled — it was silk in pastel colours with long loose streamers — she told me later she spent some time in the second toilet hiding from one of the mistresses. I didn't stay for the barbecue for the hangers-on, held at the end of the garden where it dipped sharply towards the estuary and where Rupert had his photographic studio and dark room, the size of a small house. There the mistress temporarily conceded defeat and went home and Bee and Rupert stayed or drove away.

I thought of the housecleaning, small corner by small corner, like a rug made of granny squares, when Bee rang me recently to say she was in a small flat which she had just cleaned from top to bottom. 'It's terribly small, darling' — her speech was liberally sprinkled with *darling* and *dear heart* and mine with *love* and *my dear,* like a Cockney ticket-collector. Perhaps these words were just to give us time to think. 'It took me just one can of Vim.'

The break with Rupert had been weeks before and she had lived at first with friends. I had a rumour of the break from a publisher but there had been rumours and breaks before. 'It's serious,' he said over dinner, looking pleased to be mysterious, the way people will when their information is a little hotter off the press. 'This time it's lawyers and settlements. Fighting talk.'

It didn't sound like Bee, who I knew was soft at heart but with a professional carapace: in how many plays had I seen her — she played often in a small theatre which the audience entered by walking across the stage — poised and absorbed in a character, making perfect motions for a good quarter of an hour before the non-existent curtain went up.

Sometimes she was writing — she specialised in women poets and novelists — and I wondered what it was she wrote. One night I even picked up her walking stick — the role was a game poetess, lame in one leg — and limped into her dressing room where I think she looked surprised to see me with *her* prop. But first I checked the table where she had written furiously in a final paroxysm

> RABBIT
> RABBIT
> RABBIT.

We had corresponded too. Erratically but with a good deal of fervour. She was in London sometimes or travelling with Rupert in Germany. Rupert had a liking for Sweden: it was where he first got his idea for nudes in the landscape. Once we shared a room in London.

Bee had been staying in Islington. We had both travelled on the same flight, leaving a distraught Rupert to his Leicas and a series of society portraits about which his language was unprintable. Bee came across and joined me after a quarrel with her hosts. Luckily the friends I was staying with were friends of hers too.

I remember I bagged the bed and Bee had to have the top bunk. The bottom bunk was occupied by a meccano set and other claims to possession of a ten-year-old boy. I thought he vacated it with considerable grace.

I made all this clear to Bee a few minutes after she arrived. Travelling brings out the worst, they say, and it had made me spinsterish: it's amazing how living out of a suitcase stunts your horizon. She cleared a small corner of the bottom bunk and sat on it, a wine glass in her hand.

'I don't mind at all, darling. Just as long as I don't have to share with the bloody cat.' The cat had been resuscitated by the owner of the house and they had spent a night chest-to-chest — a macabre story which he told with the relish of a scientist explaining conduction — the cat against his chest, two furs, one large heart (I imagined a valentine) against a smaller grateful one. Resuscitated and ruined, it now leapt at anyone's chest.

'I'll check before we go to sleep.'

'Would you? I rather hate cats.'

'It seems a high price to pay for survival.'

'Being neurotic, you mean?'

The room had one tiny high-up window, like a casement. I think it had leaded panes. Bee flung it open and stood on a stool to look out.

'It's a tennis court. Listen. You can hear the balls.'

Her body seemed half in and half out the window. I could just see her below the waist, like Alice. She seemed to be addressing someone.

'. . . very sick . . . not quite the thing . . . your understanding I'm sure . . .'

When I finally got it worked out, it seemed she was referring to me.

'Desperately ill, I'm afraid . . . if you could just move . . . or play more softly . . .'

I could hear a murmur of voices; it sounded like a huddle. Then the words 'tournament . . . last semi-final . . .'

'Yes, yes,' I heard her say. 'Most kind. So British.'

I marvelled later how she controlled them with her voice: soft and flexible, like a caged lark's on the surface, it had a touch of stentorian Lady Bracknell underneath. I think they must have felt that and changed courts. For the truth was that Bee could be anything she wanted.

I didn't see Bee for a long time after that but I followed her progress on stage. She was making the transition from fluffy heroine to demi-mondaine with ease. Her beauty was the self-renewing kind which I thought it had to be with Rupert. For he had struck some grim patches: some of his prints were destroyed in a fire and an art school critic accused him of plagiarism — I think it was Diane Arbus; he lost a favourite camera overboard from a luxury yacht. He had none of Bee's resilience and she frequently returned from rehearsal or performance at the theatre to comfort him. It must have been heavy work after learning lines.

I noticed he seemed happiest in the ascendant. It is a human characteristic, like living out of suitcases. Didn't Schopenhauer say it takes an angel to rejoice in another's success? I think Rupert began to dally a bit.

But all this was far away and gradual then: after the 'dying woman' act I had a miraculous recovery and we did some things together: theatres, tea at the Savoy (with Bee in tennis shoes and a long trailing tiger's tail of a scarf) and one memorable evening at an elegant home near a canal, where Bee lay under the table, bemoaning Rupert like a lovesick dog. In the end she finished off several bottles of red plonk by herself and had to be taken home rolled up in a light Arabian carpet.

Her progress down the stairs — I remember a long gallery we carried her along, our host at one end and myself and someone else at the other, and then a flight of stairs which ended in the garden which was lit by lanterns — all this remains in my mind as one of those immovable images, both radiant and very still. And our movement was the movement of Bee's own life, a sort of brilliant backtracking.

*   *   *   *

I was always quite good at writing sympathy letters. The sympathy letters that didn't seem to offer sympathy at all but continued on where we had left off at some meeting in the past, with no disaster intervening. The disaster, desertion, divorce (I never attempted death) was enclosed in a welter of everyday detail. It was the best use of existentialism — I don't know whether Jean-Paul Sartre caused these effects or whether he simply observed them in others. In one letter to a friend suffering abandonment I described a bush walk I had taken that week with as much care as Seurat putting a jigsaw together.

I doubted those letters later, when I became a candidate for my own coals of fire, but I think Bee must have been the only person to receive several. *Concentrate on your work*, I urged her, my anxiety breaking through my careful descriptions of whatever landscape I thought suitable, urban probably — Bee was a city person. *It truly is one of the great stabilities*. I don't know what the others were: keeping goldfish perhaps. *Spoil yourself* was the next step. *Go to bed with a box of chocolates and a thriller*.

Bee was at the time in an unemployment queue in London,

an out-of-work actress among methos. It was not dishonourable but demoralising. She had auditioned for a television series with '*a desperate gaiety*' she wrote; she had lost, since Rupert's departure at midnight, without even a note, ten kilograms and her clothes hung on her. Coupled with being a colonial, she felt she had nothing to lose. She could no more have afforded a box of chocolates than a trip to the Bahamas.

Yet perhaps I consoled her, perhaps there were one or two sincere phrases, not quite under my control, or she was generous enough to see in all my fakery an intention which I couldn't hide: I genuinely wanted to cheer her, and indignation, descriptive powers and flights of lyricism just meant she read the underlying intention. She was generous enough to do that and forget the chaff. It's not so easy for me: what writer wants his or her intention to be the whole subject, like looking for truffles from the top of a tree?

But Bee was resilient. Her heart might be breaking but each day she played a reckless widow with a sports car who allowed herself to be pursued by a gigolo. She allowed him to drive the sports car, which he crashed (they used a dummy), and to rob her blind but in the last episode — there were six, with the possibility of a second series — the gigolo fell in love with her. It was exactly the sort of role, she told me later, which enabled her to work out her own problems.

She sat at the dining table in the little flat, not much bigger than a couple of cupboards, bought by an aunt's legacy, and cried with great gasping sobs. It was like her Eliza in *My Fair Lady*, the anguished howl of a girl who doesn't want to speak proper. As usual, after the first few minutes, she watched herself: her rib cage swelled out like a bellows, the sobs were made by her breath. She got up and walked around: it was like a tiny stage on which she must try to appear big: wide gestures and small steps. Her hands clenched and she noticed one nail was split.

Rupert has a bad track record, people had told her. *He's a serial man. He has a new woman for each new series.* She thought of his pursuit, so overwhelming, cancelling not only their pasts — both had lurid patches — but the present — both had present lovers — as well. He was the only man she knew who could do that. He was like John the Baptist: seven veils were quite useless.

They met at a party in Earls Court and the wooing began the moment their eyes met. She never poured herself another drink; he took charge of everything; deciding the moment they should sleep together — it was a long time later she realised his flat had a 'prepared' look with just the right amount of casualness. He gave her his problems and it was like breakfast on a tray with daisies. And he told her all about his other women: he made them seem a gallery. They were like a daisy chain, stem after pierced stem and another stem through it and she, the centre of it, was something different. A long-stemmed rose had fallen through the air — she saw it coming down — stem straight out, like a saint descending; he gave up the others as though they were bread and butter.

Soon they were walking hand in hand, except Rupert was wearing a camera. But Bee was adding her eyes; they were to be the first photographs of a new series, dedicated to her. *Love & Brick*. Bare trees against tower blocks. Tower blocks and birches reflected in a canal. The headiness of love against a tombstone.

They would commute, they decided. Bee would paint the bedroom primrose, then after six months and another of Rupert's shows they would be back in the little flat. It was a perfect image for the two hemispheres of the world: a tiny box at the centre of things, where there were vast parks and spaces for crowds to gather when the need arose: a spacious open house with a golden kitchen, where the most that happened was the landscape.

Bee found work straight away at a small theatre with a talented dictatorial director. Her overseas experience gave her several leading roles and a choice of plays. Articles about her appeared in women's magazines. She was unfailingly kind to younger actresses.

Rupert's *Love & Brick* was not quite the success he had hoped but he had a promising commission for a book which involved travelling. Bee was only too happy to stay and rearrange the house which tenants had left in a mess. She tried a dab of dark red at one corner of the kitchen but it only looked like a scimitar that had drawn blood.

Letters came from her in a round handwriting. '*Darling, I'm such a poor correspondent. Did you know Rupert, dashing as he is, is scared to gut a fish? He says it turns his stomach. Poor darling! I'm learning so much, we both are — we'll be two professionals, at least that's the idea. Or two cuckoos in the same clock. Turn and turn about is the motto. Poor lamb, his show has been a bit slow. They don't understand his work so well here. The critics were a bit boorish. He says it's just his turn, the tall poppy syndrome, he calls it. Sticking out above the mower. He is being a brave pet.*'

I didn't read the words so much as look at the writing: it was firm and somehow fluffy at the same time, if writing could be fluffy. It was all arms flung around necks and faces nuzzling into collarbones, tendrils of hair lightly across a cheek. Rupert's handwriting was all spikes, as sharp as railings in a London square. He could have caught Sir Thomas More's head on an upstroke. And his words had such huge gaps between them, winds could whistle through. No word in Bee's was solitary. I had written a poem, 'Epithalamium for B and R', and she pinned it over the dab of red paint. The bedroom too had traces of other colours showing through, where the dresser had scraped and a patch of brown showed a tiny flake of turquoise. It may have been the thought of commuting but her ideas for the house became less radical. At what stage would the bedroom walls need stripping? She had located a third colour, a dusky pink, under her fingernail.

I didn't see her very often and the letters were few. Months, maybe a year, went by. Then on a visit to see a publisher I got one of the last cancellations for a Feydeau farce. I've always loved farce: the timing in it that leads to pitch and from then on you are floating. It usually comes when you can laugh no more, when you are not certain whether laughter is what you are doing, when each new word causes a sado-masochistic ache. They had hit on a novel presentation as well: the characters were in glass boxes, like telephone kiosks, down each of the far aisles. Each was as still as a waxwork and they stayed there during the interval when some people pressed their faces against the glass or tried to get them to smile. I was coming out when I saw Bee in her box. She had a black ribbon around her throat with a cameo dead centre and her hair was piled high with a few escaping curls. There was no one too close as I passed and our eyes met. She closed one eye in just the tiniest wink and by a small nod I indicated I would see her later.

I found her in her dressing room smearing cold cream liberally and swearing and laughing with two other actresses. I thought how like a sports pavilion it was; only the harsh lights and the naked bulbs and the greasy smells made it different. She was putting on a collection of odd garments, a tracksuit and a long cardigan which came to her knees and a long scarf. It was midwinter and if you breathed out you had a speech balloon.

'Drink, darling? I could do with one.'

There was a little pub two blocks away, grimy and shabby; it was one they used to frequent. We sat in the back lounge bar and ordered shandies. 'It's all I can afford. Pay day tomorrow.'

Bee drank two in quick succession. 'God, I'm tired. It's not just the play. I truly believe I'm bone tired. At least my bones ache.'

'You were wonderful, Bee. You all were. That wonderful timing.'

'It's like being on a treadmill, one of those ones with mice going faster and faster. All the costumes are fastened with Velcro, you know, that's if they get fastened at all. Half the time I'm not sure I'm done up at the back. We don't walk, we run.'

'There's no real character development, is there? That's why it's so fast, so the audience won't notice. Like those people whose diaries are always full.'

'It's my protection at the moment, darling. Keep busy. On stage and off. You haven't heard about Rupert then?'

I assured her I hadn't.

'Do you think we could have a port now. I feel like a port.'

'Any port in a storm.'

'Is that a toast? You know he's supposed — people always told me, took me aside and kindly warned me "Rupert goes through a new woman with every new series" — well, he's gone through me it seems.'

'You mean he's run off?'

'Oh no, he hasn't run off, darling. He's simply never home. It's as though he can't stop travelling. Do you think travelling could be a kind of diarrhoea?'

'You get diarrhoea when you're travelling. Sorry, I'm being facetious.'

'Feydeau is so trying, especially when it's Feydeau at home as well. I simply don't know his movements. If I ask him to talk, he simply says there's nothing wrong and I'm imagining things. He says I'm overwrought. I'm horribly tired.'

Even the port hadn't brought much colour back. Her skin, bare of makeup and pinched by the cold, then thawed by port, looked as though it had been over-exercised, slapped around by a masseuse.

'The worst thing, whenever he does show up, he expects everything to be absolutely normal. And that includes me. And I don't feel normal.'

'Is he there tonight?'

'I don't know until I get there. He was away for the weekend, he'll be back sometime this week, I guess. There's been an awful breakdown in communication.'

'Would you like me to come back with you? I can easily not go to the hotel. I could come in with you in the morning when you go?'

'Would you? You make me feel as though I had a private life.'

'Not much of a private life.'

'I was dreading the long drive, you know. Sometimes after a performance my hands shake and I nearly go to sleep at the wheel.'

Her Mini Minor was parked one street back near the theatre; it hadn't seemed worthwhile moving it. It was colder now and stiller, if that was possible. Her little car was isolated when we turned into the street, lending credence to her story.

'Here, throw this around you. I haven't got a heater.'

We drove through endless flat suburbs under the sodium

lights. Great forecourts of garages with luminous price tickets and tight, high-basemented, brick houses which no lace curtain could cheer. There were few gardens, just the occasional lemon tree or trampoline.

'I've always wondered why Rupert didn't move. It surely must be inconvenient for him as well.'

'He loves the bush and the privacy. These suburbs are practically blue with petrol fumes some mornings. It's the same blue as Paris.'

'Do you like it? Being in the bush?'

'I hardly have the time these days to enjoy it. I hardly have time to run down to the studio. I telephone him when a meal is ready. Sometimes I've left for the theatre before he comes up.'

'Is he working on a series or something? Does he seem very preoccupied?'

'He's doing bread-and-butter fashion, as he calls it. Models in industrial sites and so on. He's abstracted but it's with me.'

I could see she wasn't looking forward to arriving. The landscape had improved though. It began to dip and then run downhill, it felt exhilarating even in the dark. In the light I remembered there were no pavements from here on, just grass verges and houses tucked away in among the trees, the same distance from the road as bathing huts.

'We're nearly there. Did you finish painting the bedroom?'

'Primrose, you mean? I'm thinking of painting it again. Rupert says he's sick of it. That's another thing, he's taken to sleeping some nights in his studio.'

There were no lights. Bee eased the Mini Minor down the steep drive and parked it under the house. Under the house was never finished; it went in next to a concrete mixer and a pile of planks; I marvelled again at her wedding clean-up.

'Wait here and I'll go and put some lights on.'

I saw her go up the steps with a pocket torch and shine the light on the keyhole. The light came on and I followed.

The kitchen was as bright as I ever remembered: nothing would dim it. It was like stepping into a grapefruit. Dishes lay around on the sink and a can of baked beans with a jagged lid, a half-full milk bottle.

'Come through and I'll make us some coffee.'

The big lounge room was bathed in a blue light and there were stripes of moonlight on the rugs.

'I'll just sit down for a minute and get my breath.'

'I'll make the coffee, you stay there.'

I found instant coffee and a papier-mâché tray with blue and red flowers. I sniffed the milk and it seemed okay.

'Won't be a minute, Bee.'

But when I got back she was asleep. So soundly, my hand on her shoulder failed to rouse her. I got a rug from one of the beds and covered her and lifted her feet onto a bean bag. Then I sat beside her and drank my coffee. Slowly, looking out in the direction of the estuary.

* * * *

My own career as a writer was not so spectacular nor so fraught as Bee's. She told me later each new poster advertising her name, usually higher than the rest, seemed obliterated by the poster that followed; in between each success, each first night's tremulous bow, there was a pit which made any real pit in a theatre the merest simile. Each time she entered her dressing room it seemed not hers, or hers by virtue of wiles and technique and knowing where to place her head. Her portfolio of photographs — she was naturally photogenic — were from the best angles and in the most flattering light. 'Darling,' she would say, because she had no reservations and regarded herself as a canvas, 'it's getting fuzzier and fuzzier. Like the Impressionists.'

'Like Turner,' I would add. '*London Bridge*.'

'Oh, Turner's sepulchral. He's just longing for people to fall in the Thames. Perhaps they have, but who would see them in all that fog?'

I often noticed when she performed how graciously she drew attention to her best features; slender ankles, a columnar neck which always looked younger than her face, instead of the reverse which was usual — 'it must be my vocal chords' — her cloud of hair, so versatile and always threatening to spill over like the froth on ale. When we went to tea at the Savoy, when she leaned out the window, she was still the actress: she knew how to command her due. But I sometimes wondered if, attending so constantly to the surfaces, as though the world was lit by 200 watt bulbs, it didn't give her an extra vulnerability. And she could always look so wonderful, so blooming, when she was in absolute pain.

I can see her at a party, holding a glass with ice in it which clinked because she was shaking ever so slightly, but it was the only sign; she was like a girl at the beginning of an affair, not the end. She did the same at the end of her telephone calls, which could last an hour, went off with a *Dear heart, All the love in the world, My precious* and you felt the spine stiffen and the hauling up of morale. I wonder if actresses do have this special relationship to words, like a carthorse to sugar. The rest of us want to dig deeper, or let words alone, but Bee would aver words were exactly what they said. I think she went further and thought what they said was essential.

I think it was this opposite way with words which drew us together. I was brain-aching and effacing and tougher inside than you might think; she was daring and existentialist and as soft inside as a marshmallow. Perhaps that is why I wrote the Bluebeard letter.

None of his friends actually thought Rupert would be faithful. Perhaps that's why someone asked the minister if he was unfrocked. Frocked or unfrocked, I doubt if the questioner was much reassured. I listened to the old-fashioned vows and wished them power and at the same time knew the power they had was in the heart of the partakers. I had gone to mass with Bee the week before and she had taken communion; she would so much have preferred a priest. Perhaps Rupert might have been nonplussed by a priest. And Rupert's look was so attentive, so wholly concentrated, as though he'd taken over Bee's existentialism and made it his own. It was that impression of Rupert's that gave me my first intimation of chill.

A writer's life has its disappointments too. In fact they are rather steady. I think I determined at the beginning to train myself for them. I wanted to be able to open rejection slips with a Buddha-like calm. Sometimes I was so reined in, I forgot to celebrate the odd bit of success. I began to see that these Eastern gods flatten everything. Sometimes I thought what Bee would have done and it was the opposite and it made me laugh. She was becoming '*overexposed*' she wrote; she was thinking of branching into radio or even writing; Rupert was working on a particularly difficult project, he needed more of her support. I think I wrote then urging her to go on and not worry about the over-exposure. '*Surely it is the audience who decides, not the producer.*' I didn't think my naivety worried her any more than I was swept away by pet names. '*Rupert is in some kind of crisis,*' she wrote back, some months later. '*I really feel I need to take time off. I can always go back.*'

I thought of my Buddhism, which had signally failed to cope with the rejection of a book of short stories I had laboured over for months. I had mastered envelopes, not packages. '*Would Rupert do this for you?*' I wrote.

It was partly my anger for the rejection but I saw Rupert's malaise as a kind of sabbatical; I had never known him to be threatened by crisis at any really crucial time. He seemed to be making an awful lot of the creative process. I was looking at a photograph of Thom Gunn, whom I greatly admired. It was a sinister photograph with a careful charm. The poet was boldly tattooed on the arms and a large bird, perhaps gull, perhaps albatross, hung from its wingtips behind him; he was wearing black leather and chains. Yet the poems open on the desk, I guess they were in that stage known as drafts, were of a pristine neatness. A con man, I thought. There is no fine carelessness in what you value.

I had a suspicion Rupert's malaise was of this order: it came in his holidays; I had never known it to spoil an exhibition. '*He's suffering so much,*' Bee wrote, but her own suffering, the loss of a part she had always wanted to do, something that had been a showpiece for her in London and she could now introduce to the Antipodes — what an extra kind of curtain call that would be, even more secure than 'actress' — that went to someone else, someone she coached in the evenings between being Rupert's ghost. His *mal de mer* (this was how he described it) had made him very silent and the silence hung between them. The yellow kitchen when I called that second winter reminded me of the yellow lines in the Immigration queues at Los Angeles airport. A whisper had gone down the line that you crossed them at your peril and since the police were armed, no one dared.

But there was one commission Bee could not abandon: it involved some taping and it had to be done in London, together with some additional filming. She was bound to it by contract and as the day of her departure approached, her tension and misery seemed to me unbearable. I couldn't help thinking Rupert was playing her like a fish and when I heard rumours of a former mistress, the one who had lingered at the barbecue, I forgot all my Buddhism in an instant. For hadn't Bluebeard inculcated the very suspicions in his wives that he accused them of? Happy, they might have regarded the little locked room as nothing more than a place for storing the vacuum cleaner or a second place for washing the hands. He made it *glow*. Rupert who had overwhelmed her by the present, was now obliterating her with the past. A true Bluebeard never quite allows the last corpse to lose its phosphorescence until a new victim is on the way to being installed. I think I got quite lyrical, with the lyricism of one who invents and discovers these things at the moment of writing. '*Write as you think*,' I told my class of WEA students that year. '*Don't think before you pick up the pen*.' I had certainly saved up a good deal.

It was a premature letter because there were reconciliations to come and more liaisons and more sudden plummeting depressions like knife stabs in Shakespeare. But it influenced Bee enough for her to carry it in her handbag and during one of their reconciliations Rupert saw it.

I regretted it in a way. It put me down among the forgotten corpses in Bluebeard's cupboard, those who were reduced to a hank of hair and a pile of bones, a few tatters of cloth. I had declared my hand but I told myself I was forced into it, by friendship certainly, but also by romanticism. If I didn't believe in it for myself — I envisaged no garden ceremony in my wildest fantasies, with everything just perfect — I expected them to hold because of all the effort that had gone into theirs. Letting that go was harder by far than being a Buddhist over envelopes. It was one of the problems the envelopes led to.

It was my one punishing outburst and for quite a while it punished the relationship between us. Whoever said frankness clears the air was a liar. It clears it of everything soft and conciliatory and you see the weapons ranged against you. After the letter I could only be a partial confidante: otherwise everything was fine. '*We are reconciled,*' Bee wrote, in her round looping letters. '*We are going to Greece for a new series. Rupert wants to do something different. I'm going to work half the year and spend the rest making Greek salads. What Rupert admires in me, he tells me, is my real understanding of the artistic temperament.*' Ranged behind my Bluebeard's letter I could only be on the side of the devil. What did Rupert know of the artistic temperament, I thought; but I wrote, aping her names, '*I hope you'll be very happy, darling.*'

Then for a time there was nothing, not even a postcard. I was writing the first draft of a novel; I was up to my neck in mire. I told myself I had always had an actressy friend, that they were replaceable, that they were some deficiency in my character, like the ghost in Hamlet's. What right did I have to advise. Months passed. I decided I would never have another actressy friend. And one day I would sit down and analyse where I had gone wrong so I could profit from it.

I remember the night Bee rang. It was cold and in September. I think it was around 6 p.m. 'Dear heart, I've got to see you. We've finally split. Where can we meet? Give me a time and a place.'

I named a bar near the theatre where I had gone backstage holding on to a stick. It was modern and light with lime-green walls and chrome chairs. Its food was a jungle behind glass like an aquarium and whatever you ordered was heated in a microwave oven. But it was new and modern, a break from the past.

'Frightful, isn't it? But the coffee's quite good.'

'Do you mind if I get something to eat? I haven't had anything since this morning.'

I bought a slice of underdone beef, which twirled for a second to melt a tablespoon of gravy over it, and a piece of wilting lettuce. Bee fished for a prawn cocktail in the greenery and some potato salad and a roll.

'I'm sure it's hideous but I don't care. I don't feel as though I care about anything.' I looked at her in alarm but she looked bright-eyed. 'Not care in the sense of free, light-headed. I'm like the lady who was peeling carrots and thought to herself, *Scrape, scrape, scrape.*'

'What have you been doing? Rehearsing?'

'Researching actually. I'm writing a play myself and I'm reading up the background.'

'Do you want to talk about it?'

'No. I've been doing it all day. I want to talk about splitting.'

'It always sounds like banana split.'

'If only it was that simple. Remember you said Rupert was a Bluebeard?'

'I'd rather I hadn't . . .'

'It comforted me at the time. I used to carry your letter inside my bra like a tramp stuffed with newspapers. I'm wise to you, I'd think. I've seen the key. Well this time he's broken out of the pattern. He's gone off with a young model and he's photographing her in the nude from helicopters all over the place. Sometimes it's with animals, a pen of sheep and she lies down in the middle of them — they get the farmer's permission first naturally; sometimes it's giant pipes or the top of a ridge. Rupert says I'm insane to be jealous but

I know they're having an affair. He just laughs because the evidence is so tiny.'

'What do you mean, the evidence?'

'The photographs. It's like looking down at a starfish, a terribly well-delineated starfish. Sometimes he gets ten acres into a shot. I could bear his past ladies somehow, it was like someone dropping stitches in knitting and catching up, but this is so foreign. So I walked out and here I am. Lawyers, the whole thing. It's all poisonous, I can tell you.'

'You really think he's in love with this starfish person? You don't think it's just an artistic obsession?'

'My dear, do you think there is any such thing? I've been through all that. The eternally fresh innocence of the creative. It's all bullshit. Utter bullshit.'

Several people at nearby tables were looking at us curiously. Bee was waving her arms about rather a lot and when she was not doing that, she was ferociously making pellets out of her bread roll.

'Let's have some more coffee. I'll get it.'

When I came back, she was lighting a cigarette and looking at the nails of her left hand.

'You've taken your ring off.'

'I threw it at him actually. Told him to have it fitted through the starfish's nose — see if he could catch a glimpse of gold. Oh, we had a fine fight. I dragged up absolutely everything. I don't know where the ring went, it rolled under the table, I think. I threw all his photography books on the floor. He said that I had never respected him. All the plays I gave up for him, to nurse his wounded ego. I could spit.'

'When did all this happen?' The writer of letters which people wore inside their bras, I was beginning to sound like a reporter.

'Two weeks ago. I've buried myself since then. You're the first person I've seen outside work.'

'Why did you write RABBIT, RABBIT, RABBIT on the pad on the stage? I always meant to ask.'

'I'd been reading Updike or I was as scared as a rabbit, I can't remember. I know it had some significance at the time. I think sometimes I changed it, it gave me something to look forward to.'

'What strange creatures actresses are.'

'Not strange really. Always trying to prove we're human. That's what the rabbit was about really. Just because you've got a well-modulated voice and know how to hold your head . . . people think all your feelings must be superficial. Rupert thinks I'm superficial, he thinks my anguish is nothing.'

She lowered her head suddenly and sobbed, some of her hair tangled with a lettuce leaf. I moved my plate with its gravy stains like exhumation marks. I put my hand on her shoulder and willed her to be Lady Bracknell. After a moment or two she was. She blew her nose sternly and patted her eyes. Then she got out a handmirror and with total concentration patted on compressed powder and drew a new cupid's bow over her lips. The thin underfilled mouth of Colette, with its cruel corners, was in that year, in very dark reds.

'I've got this little flat belonging to an old lady for six months. It's so stuffed with furniture I can hardly move. But it suits me. I have to look after her canary.'

'I expect it's yellow, this canary.'

'No, blue-green. It matches the sofa.'

Any moment we'd be laughing and I'd be following her into the Savoy, football scarf and sneakers. 'I think we can bring this off, darling. Stay close.' In the event we just swept in. When we came out she was twirling a small cardboard box secured with a ribbon. It contained the choux pastry she hadn't eaten. Inside her windcheater were two serviettes and two teaspoons. '*Down and Out in Paris and London*,' she said. 'Have you read that?' I had but I'd never hoped to put it into practice. What use were my notes, my wild similes compared to her experience?

'How often do you have to clean its cage?'

'I've no idea. When it smells, I suppose. I had pet mice once, they were worse than Sunday School. I wonder what Rupert's doing?'

'Have you seen him since?'

'I thought I saw him once. And I phoned once and hung up. I felt like the phantom deep-breather.'

'You must hold on, Bee, you and the canary.'

I never learned. I think exhortations must have been bred in me. I was like one of those violent movies on TV where they shoot first on a rescue mission.

'Promise me something, Bee. Promise you'll ring once a week.'

I had a vision of myself as a therapist: one hour every Thursday. I could give her the dialogue in advance. '*You're bound to feel depressed. It's only natural. You must make allowances. Clean out the canary. It could be worse.*'

It was getting dark and we sat over our coffee cups and from time to time Bee pushed a bit of salad around her plate.

'I really must get back. I'm auditioning tomorrow. I don't really care if I get the part or not.'

'How did you come?'

'I've got my bike.'

'Have you got lights?'

'Yes. I've got all sorts of bits and pieces to attach to myself as well.' She fumbled in her holdall and brought out something that looked like a luminous handcuff. 'It goes around the ankle. Rupert shan't get rid of me so easily.'

We parted at the door and I walked slowly off in search of a cab. When I turned back all I could see of Bee was the luminous glow of fireflies as they made their way up the road.

*   *   *   *

For a few weeks Bee was as good as her word. She rang each week, usually Thursday or Friday. Sometimes her voice positively sang, 'I've cleaned the canary and guess what I've been offered, a film part. I'm so busy, darling, I don't know how I ever had time for Rupert. I hear he's going around with a long face . . .' Sometimes it was about lawyers. 'I'm changing my lawyer, she's advised reconcilia-tion, she's too soft.' But when she went to a tough one, his penetrating questions made her recoil. 'He wants me to lay it on the line exactly what I want.' Rupert had written and there were flowers in the letterbox. She recognised the gypsophila which grew by the back door. That week when he phoned, she hung up.

I thought his tactics were unfair and said so. I talked about clean breaks as though I was a bone surgeon. I seized on clichés as though I was writing a death certificate. I counselled on the phone as though it was a late night show. We were two voices but our words didn't meet in the middle. Sometimes a month would go by and I would hear rumours.
— Bee's looking ten years younger, everyone says so.
— Rupert's threatening to commit suicide. He looks a hundred.
— Bee's sleeping with a producer.
— Rupert's run off with a waitress.

Rupert's *Landscape With Nude* show opened and was a great success. But the young model, chastely clothed in black, did not appear on his arm; she was with her fiancé. In most of the photographs she would have fitted comfortably on to a postage stamp. Still Bee was right, there was something very well defined about her. Even her fingertips seemed stretched out and a tiny pinpoint indicated each nipple. Rupert looked haggard and interesting but I noticed he seemed to be avoiding being seen with any particular woman.

Bee too seemed involved with no one. She bicycled everywhere and left the theatre chastely every night to cook supper with her canary. But she was looking visibly stronger. I caught a glimpse of her across a room at a party. She was wearing a black dress with shoe-string straps and her hair was in a new style, very full on top and cropped around the ears. She pushed her way over and we sat in a window seat clutching our g & ts.

'You're looking fabulous, Bee. It suits you, this single life.'

'This celibate life. I'm getting fat.'

'Perhaps you are a little plumper. No one would notice.'

'Except the wardrobe mistress. She's having to let my costumes out. I'm not her favourite person.'

'You got the part then? The one you were mentioning.'

'Yes. I didn't really want it. They say I gave the most relaxed audition.'

It was for one of the sisters in Chekhov, the eldest, the one who has headaches and at the finale stands in the centre, slightly raised on a pedestal. The one who says '*How we have suffered, sisters*' or words to that effect.

The room was full of people and the record player was going, a primitive beat that could only be assuaged by drinking or dancing. We were too close to the bar for comfort.

'Do you feel like a walk in the garden? It's not cold.'

'Why not. It'll clear my head, I expect.'

'I'll just get my shawl.'

There was nowhere to walk really. Just down the drive. Our high heels made us wobble on the stones. There was a tree half way down and a patch of grass. 'Let's sit down here. You're not frightened of catching a chill?'

'I knew a girl who caught a chill and bled right through the mattress. I don't think that's likely to happen to me. You don't think I'm looking fat?'

'No, honestly. You look luxurious. You should be a kept woman, Bee. A sheik perhaps.'

'What about you?'

'I'd like a sugar daddy to buy me typewriter ribbons and reams and reams of A4. In return I'd go to dinner with him once a week and be gracious.'

'He wouldn't be satisfied with that.'

'He wouldn't get anything more. I'd be merciless.'

There was a pause and she plucked a bit of grass.

'How are you really?'

'Not bad, I think. There's been no contact for months now. A determined policy of not answering the phone and returning letters unopened.'

I was amazed at her bravery; it wasn't like her not to respond to a cue.

'And the lawyer. Are you still with the same one?'

'He says he's going to nail Rupert to a lamp post and deliver his hide. So he says.'

'And how do you feel about it?'

'I don't know. I don't know anything any longer. Do you really think I look all right?'

'You look wonderful. You look on top of the world. Surely you know that. When you cross a room . . .'

'It's funny, you know, but that never works when you're

an actress. It's like words for you, I suppose. The tricks that are so good on stage only leave you uneasy off it. I go on acting, like at this party, but my heart's not in it.'

'I went to a dinner party once where they talked about words. It really got quite heated. I wanted to scream out *"But words are to use!"* '

'I catch myself listening attentively to some man and I know it's just an angle of the head, a look in the eye . . . I can be miles away, someone inside my own picture. When Rupert was there it wasn't so frightening. He has his camera to hide behind. We balanced.'

'But he was so difficult, so hateful to you. That time he disappeared leaving you without money . . . You can't go back, Bee. It must be better to go forward.'

'I know. I've already had two offers. One at this party tonight.'

'Oh, Bee. You sound so mournful.'

'I don't mean to. It's just that this growing stronger is so painful.'

A car turned into the drive and we moved back against the hedge. Its beam swept our faces and the moment the light touched us I knew Bee was the star. I caught a head turning and a look of interest.

'Perhaps we'd better go back.'

'To words and angles of the head.'

'You can have some of my angles.'

'You can have any of my words.'

We hobbled up the drive, more unsteady than when we came down. It's fatal to stop moving in some kinds of heels.

And that was the last I saw of her. In the tacit agreement people have when they've shared a confidence, or even a shadow of one, we separated at the door and if we circulated, it was on different sides of the room. From time to time I caught an angle of the head and thought she looked attentive and she must have guessed I was using words in their proper carelessness. I felt more and more like a therapist who has taken someone for a session that lasts as long as a cigarette smoked in a lull on a verandah. I might at some future time make a writer but I could never have been an actress: I knew nothing about the limitations of will. I thought that a transference of optimism, even a holding steadiness, could be made simply by conduction. Like the woman who bled through the mattress, it was meant to prove something. But Bee was right about angles.

I was working on a collection of short stories. None of them seemed to have any kernel. It was as though real life were rushing past, angles, words, A to B, and it was impossible to fix it to anything. Bee's appearance encouraged me but I didn't have any evidence; Rupert at least had a shape in his lens, the starfish woman. I almost began to see what he was doing. Bluebeard's problem was he wasn't really transportable. Or about as transportable as a pop band. I wondered what Bee would find.

One of the stories had been singled out for comment; I decided to start there. I wrote the beginning over and over again, refining it. The characters were in danger of disappearing. There was something I felt I didn't know about them. I was so engrossed I missed the Chekhov but I heard it was overdressed. Bee in dove grey had been a model of soft sacrifice. Rupert's show was over and there was talk of it touring; a Japanese critic had been impressed.

One day I dug out of my notes the poem I had written for their wedding. I think I intended it for a wedding present.

> *Out of the dust strike*
> *A satiny note, a shaft*

Bee had fastened it to the yellow kitchen wall where it had become spattered and damp.

> *Where the light meets*
> *Resistance and conclusion*

It brought back their wedding and then like a Seurat its dissolution into shimmering, elongated flecks of colour, with the yellow over it all like the sun.

> *And forgets to move on*
> *Bemused into abeyance*
> *Of all else that is trivial*
> *Inanimate and soul-less.*

The kitchen like a scimitar and the side room with the Turkish love pillow, the token mistress, omen of things to come, my Bluebeard letter and becoming partisan, our two worlds of words and angles. And I expected Bee to rise out of all this like a phoenix.

> *And this note is*
> *A sort of herald*
> *Whirling quiet squares*
> *And plane trees patient*
> *As caged birds, a quiet river*
> *Mating in its bed*
> *Into proportionate animation*
> *Through a sense of sight.*

We were in winter again. It was almost time for the lady to return and claim the canary. Some of the actors and actresses were on strike; it may have been for more pay or because they were passed over by an American producer for film parts. One night I saw Bee's face on television in a picket line. She was wearing the new torn look, a loose pinafore with holes in the bodice, but she made everyone else look plain.

It was time for me to move as well. I almost didn't phone; we had practically lost contact after all. But I had half an hour to spare before my taxi came; which therapist does not wish to go out on a triumph?

She wasn't at the phone number I had; an old lady answered; it must have been the owner of the canary. I was feeling so light-headed I almost asked after the bird.

'She's moved. Just a moment and I'll find the number.'

I dialled and after about five rings she answered.

'Dear heart,' she said. 'I was just thinking of you. Remember that poem you wrote for us? I've just had it re-copied. We're buying a new house, no more painting the bedroom walls. It was about to close in on us — so many layers — *Babes in the Woods,* Rupert called it — we're out of the woods now — and you, my darling, how are you?'

I forced something back into my voice, not gaiety, I wasn't master of the angles on words, just cheerfulness and what I hoped sounded like optimism. But I felt chilled all over, and for half an hour in the bus.

'You do understand, don't you, darling? I'm not cut out to be alone . . .'

Deconstructing ❧

On the third afternoon of the conference, when Alicia Fox was resting in her chalet, she caught a movement on the track that ran below the clotheslines. She got to her feet and went to the window in time to see a head swathed in a sweatband, pale blue, and two wrists flapping, as the owner in matching blue shorts and ankle-bands went past. The face wore a concentrated, ecstatic, almost-Zen expression, while the hanging wrists were like the distracting and, some thought, single flaw in the ballerina Ulanova. Dying duck wrists, Alicia thought, with a deathly life of their own. Then the thought that this was illogical, even at an English Language and Literature Conference, made her smile. Like her, the woman in blue had obviously decided to miss a lecture and attend to something more profitable: beauty or recreation or being alone to collect her thoughts.

That morning Alicia had attended a paper on Henry Handel Richardson and tried to give it her full attention. She guessed it had been a masterly paper because there were very few questions at the end. The lecturer had an almost Byronic look, with dark wavy hair. He was dressed entirely in cream and his demeanour as he waited for questions suggested he didn't expect to be surprised. Alicia had noticed before how few academics like to venture outside their own spheres: not for them the bold sorties of the writer, who was constantly crossing minefields in a state of ignorance.

There were six writers present and one was at this moment playing his guitar in the common room, which was a separate chalet approached through an entirely ornamental arch overgrown with ivy. The tracks from the chalets — there were clusters of them dotted about in the gum trees — meandered in an artistic way and climbed little artificial hills which made the walk to breakfast peculiarly frustrating.

Each morning little knots of academics and the occasional solitary figure — representing an alternative moral tale — made their way to the big canteen where breakfast was served. Alicia had been pleased to discover two familiar faces in her chalet: a famous elder-statesman poet and his wife — they had adjoining rooms — and they usually contrived to knock as they went past and allow her to catch up. They ate at wooden tables overlooking a clearing bordered by gum trees. The grass was dry and the leaves of the gums, like small pointed tongues, lay in drifts across the paths and lawns. One of the visiting academics, a Canadian, spoke of feeling desiccated.

Alicia recognised the woman from the path in the queue. Her hair was freshly dampened and she glowed with satisfaction, as people often do a short time after exercise. Rarely after mental exercise, Alicia thought. That accounts for why most academics are in a constant state of hostility. Kill or be killed, someone had described it. Often in her year of visitor status, Alicia had felt there was some kind of ground to be held with every fibre of the being. A picture of the dying-stage defence of some American Civil War battleground, in an etching, always with dark trees and someone, who could surely have been better employed elsewhere, holding the standard in the fading light.

'Minstrel boys,' she said suddenly to the elder-statesman poet, who was sitting beside her, holding a sausage speared on a fork up before his face, to see if it would do as a lorgnette. They knew each other well enough to talk in disjointed phrases.

'Fancy yourself as one, my dear?'

'No, I was just thinking how vulnerable. Like the flag bearer. They would almost certainly be mown down.'

'Like poets among academics, my dear. The poor creatures were undoubtedly almost totally image. Not of course that they knew it themselves — that was probably a military secret decided by very old generals. But, I wonder, did one ever see a minstrel boy without a fair brow and blond curls?'

'I don't see why there shouldn't have been one with acne,' said his wife, tucking into scrambled eggs resembling custard.

'Of course one might have developed a pimple in the course of battle. Very likely. Then it would become necessary, almost, to die.'

'Clarence can't take anything seriously,' his wife said. 'It makes him exceedingly tedious.'

But Alicia was thinking there was almost always a grain of something in what he said. An irrelevant grain. He almost always set her thinking on some new tangent. His poems were like that too: on the night they read together his discourse leading to each poem became hard to distinguish from the poem itself, so closely were working notes and work intertwined.

The writers had all performed on the first night: the letter inviting them to the conference as guests had suggested they might enjoy the papers for the rest of the week. A few trips had been arranged, one to a bird sanctuary, and there was to be a formal dinner.

The readings had gone reasonably well, thanks to the presence of the elder-statesman poet, though he was a hard act to follow, and now the lecture-filled days stretched ahead, with their subjects able to be comprehended by very few. For lunch the members of the conference made their way to the staff club, a gracious Gothic building, much enlarged and sprawling, set in beautiful grounds, but the evening meal, served promptly at 5 p.m., was in the same cafeteria in which they began the day.

'Bathetic ending,' the elder statesman said, 'and yet if I don't eat, I may be forced to shoot a rabbit.'

'I fear your chances may be slim,' Alicia remarked. 'Do you fancy yourself creeping about under the gums in the moonlight?'

'Have you noticed how often images leave the inner man unsatisfied? One cannot eat a moon. The real test of poetry, if we dared, would be on the starving.'

'And they might very well eat you,' his wife remarked. 'I doubt if they'd wait for a number of stanzas.'

'We could always raid the Food Technology Laboratory. It's that long building we pass before the chalets.'

'Ah yes. For all we know it may conceal in its labyrinthine depths a small intimate room with red gingham tablecloths and candles in Vat 69 bottles. There should be a steak or two on the premises, waiting to be measured with callipers.'

Despite the earliness of the hour, dusk was falling as they made their way on the now familiar path. Only the leaves were different, glowing like fireflies. 'Come to my room for a nightcap around ten and we can talk about T. S. Eliot or Ezra Pound, whichever you prefer.'

Confident they would talk about neither, Alicia turned the key in her lock and threw up the window which she had practically closed to secure the single yellow towel they had each been issued. There had been one awful moment on the night of the reading when she had returned to the chalet to change and collect her poems. She had taken the wrong turning and climbed over the wrong hill and ended, under an identical arch, in a group of uninhabited chalets. But this had not registered for a considerable time.

She had blamed the elder statesman for locking the passage door and had climbed out on a ledge and peered in what she imagined was her window. A pristine bed and an uncovered pillow had failed to convince her and she had moved, rather precariously on the ledge like a lovesick student, peering in room after room until the truth dawned.

The cell next to hers, when she knocked a little after ten, was full of smoke from cigars and cigarettes and the built-in desk, as rigid and unwelcoming as the ironing boards at the end of each floor, was covered with bottles and glasses. A man with a red beard was seated on the bed and the elder statesman introduced him by saying, 'Felix here is giving no papers, only introducing one of the speakers. Very easy, I call it.'

'You'd be surprised how much care and nervousness goes into one of these introductions,' Felix replied. 'It's a peculiar combination of a conceit larded with compliments and an indication you are intimately familiar with his whole opus. Though you've got a hangover and are totally indifferent to his opinions, you must give the impression you've been awaiting a few words like the Second Coming.'

'Well, you'll certainly have a hangover in the morning. Perhaps they'll mistake it for emotion, if your voice trembles slightly,' said the poet's wife, rummaging in the Chillibin.

'I thought I saw someone running in the garden earlier,' Alicia said. 'A woman in a blue headband.'

'Dr Susie Sabido, UCLA, I presume,' the elder statesman said. 'A supremely gifted woman of the track and field.'

'She was running slowly, though her hand movements were quite rapid,' Alicia said.

'He's pulling your leg, of course,' Felix said. 'Dr Sabido was possibly massaging her wrists as she passed from chalet to chalet: she normally has several suitors at once. Her speciality is Jane Austen.'

'Didn't she write something on the significance of the mud on Eliza Bennet's petticoat? The state of the roads, whether Mrs Bennet could have dispatched the carriage, the length of the grasses in the fields crossed, number of worm mounds . . .'

'You make her sound like Darwin,' Alicia protested. 'How many worms are pulling Stonehenge under?'

'How many inches of mud pulled Eliza Bennet under? What range these academics allow themselves. A poet is far more strait-laced.'

'Certainly our paltry efforts give rise to considerable embroideries,' Alicia said, marvelling that such a sentence could occur after so many glasses, admittedly watered, of whisky. The window was open as far as possible and the night too had a smoky tang. 'Even buildings,' she went on, thinking of the university tower, the delicate traceries in stone, the gargoyles looking down like tiny shrunken professors.

'We are the cornerstone,' the elder statesman said. 'A rather ugly cut that you sometimes see on a brick when the trowel is not wielded properly.'

The highlight of the conference was to be the speaker on deconstruction: unfortunately, due to an aberration of the timetable, his main lecture coincided with the visit to the bird sanctuary. Alicia had caught sight of the deconstructionist walking past the dining hall with a firm step and head, surely a rather large head, with noble planes, held high. Perhaps he is a student of the Alexander technique, she thought. She had booked for the bird sanctuary at registration when they seemed to require a decision. A coloured brochure with photographs of the birds: Kaka, Kokako, North Island Brown Kiwi, had been handed out. But the journey took more than two hours in a hot bus: it was not long before Alicia was regretting the deconstructionist, who might have provided a reduction. The elder statesman, two seats behind, was evidently thinking along the same lines, as he was mopping his face with a spotted handkerchief. He was hung about with several cameras and light meters and even a water bottle.

Like all tourist spots there was a feeling of turnstiles and stopwatches: the slatted boardwalks rang with their footsteps like the Billy Goats Gruff. The birds themselves were in large cages that soared high above fully grown trees and cut the sky into wedges.

'The ownership of space above skyscrapers? What's the name for it?'

'Air space?' queried his wife.

'You know what I mean. Like a pile of books and above them rises what is ultimately more solid, a reputation.'

'Surely the owners of this air must be surprised to find they own it and that it is valuable?' An absurd idea of a little man standing on the roof of a building as high or higher than the Empire State and looking up at cumulus clouds came to mind.

'But the air space of these birds is limited, deconstructed. One feels pity for a sampling.'

They tramped on, grateful for the patches of shade and the amazing thickness of the foliage in the concealed cages.

After climbing for about three quarters of an hour, the

path began to descend and they came to a number of cages in full sunlight. The takahe's cage, since the bird was flightless, was long rather than high, enclosing what seemed to be a whole swamp. Window sections set into the wooden walls enabled them to locate one of the males standing guard over a very undistinguished nest. The takahe's colours were ragged and carelessly applied, like a bungalow in need of painting.

'To think for this we are missing a definitive Welshman deconstructing,' the elder statesman said, when he had caught up. He was mopping his face copiously with his handkerchief.

'It looks as though it's tried to colour itself in and not been able to reach everywhere,' Alicia said. Yet in spite of its failed colouring the bird was meaty, substantial. It bore their presence, surely irritating, behind its back like a cricketer on the boundary bears the remarks of a hostile crowd.

Back at the Information Centre there was just time to take tea in a little annexe and buy souvenirs. Alicia bought a calender featuring the takahe prominently and the poet's wife bought a headscarf with a border of native ferns. They were deposited back at the university just in time for the evening meal.

The formal dinner was notable for the care the women took with their appearance. Uncrushable flimsy dresses that must have been squeezed between books appeared and some that were almost backless. Alicia, who had underestimated the occasion, was a bit like the takahe and looked forward, in her simple skirt and blouse, to being seated in the same way the takahe might have wished to disappear into the scrub. The ironing boards at the end of each corridor were in demand and the atmosphere became charged like a ball. A knot of women, including the glamorous runner in a canary-yellow gown, was ahead of them on the path and the little hills rose and fell as though, in their evening sandals, they were bareback riders. The men, Alicia was relieved to see, were hardly adorned at all: evidently they considered their brains quite sufficient: one professor was still in his tweed jacket with leather elbows.

There were too many shrimp cocktails set out on the large tables and while they were seating themselves, hopeful of being included by a gesture in an interesting group, the excess cocktails were taken away by tired waitresses. Alicia found herself seated beside a handsome man and opposite an earnest woman. By the time their cocktail glasses were emptied, they were discussing Christina Stead. Alicia looked around to locate the elder statesman, who might have supplied some personal knowledge or an anecdote, but he was at a distant table. Occasional gusts of laughter showed he was successfully preserving his identity. The woman in the yellow silk was sitting with another beautiful woman; they were both leaning on their elbows.

How delightful that we have such a good subject, Alicia thought, as, without losing their conversation, they circled a cold buffet on which dishes of cold meat were arranged like tree bark. A rich author and a rich repast. They had already drunk liberally from the carafes and had them refilled. But weren't they, in attempting to discuss this author, just a little like a cat that has shot too far up a tree?

'Too prodigal for some tastes,' the woman was saying. 'Too much thrown away.'

'I'm sorry I missed the lecture on deconstruction,' Alicia said, turning to the dark-haired man. 'I was hoping for at least a definition. Is it something as rich, perhaps, as Christina Stead?'

'All theoreticians would like such richness,' he replied with a smile. 'At least at the beginning. But it will break down slowly through conferences such as this and papers into something quite threadbare.'

'In a single sentence of Christina Stead there's enough for a story, several stories. There's no fear,' the woman was saying and it struck Alicia that her examination would be scrupulous, taking infinite pains. Whereas the author . . .

Outside the lawn and the gardens, the beds and yews, had reverted to another century: Maupassant perhaps. Some of the men were lighting cigars and taking their coffee cups out on to the verandah. An absurd image of Bel-Ami came to Alicia's mind: the hut balanced on the cliff edge with the lovers inside, being rocked back and forth. The same silver light on the sea.

Miss or Ms ❧

We were standing at the Information Desk in the lunch hour, two senior librarians, one running a wand like a lighted pencil over the accession numbers and the other straightening the books on the counter so they were upside down and spines out. Keeping the desk clear was a fetish but on Mondays we never caught up. The overnight returns box, like a big wooden laundry hamper, bulged with books their owners said had been returned or never had, books found down the backs of sofas, books the family dog had taken a fantastic bite out of. We went on wanding like automatons, or at least Mercedes did — she was backup — while I answered queries.

'Have you anything on budgerigars?' a little dumpy woman with very bird-like eyes asked, and I led her off to 636.6864 between bantams and racing pigeons and dogs and cats. By the time I got back she had told me her budgie had very unusual markings: this is what libraries are, an exchange of information. Mercy was joining up a young woman and asking for a second address: 'Work, friend, neighbour, relative, someone you know well,' she prompted. I had recently found myself saying 'good friend' because it sounded warmer or more responsible, making the borrower seem more worthy. But the young woman gave a lawyer's office and a box number. There was just one more question and I knew Mercy always saved it to last: 'Would you like to be referred to as Miss or Ms?'

It's not easy to say 'Ms'. It came out 'Miz', as though, with a warm inflection, it might be short for Mitzi. Mercy is very warm and encouraging: a contestant on a quiz programme could tell which was the correct answer.

'Miss,' said the young woman, firmly.

'Are you sure?' Mercy asked.

'Quite sure,' the young woman answered and now there was no mistaking the asperity.

'Obviously she hasn't profited from a study of the law,' Mercy said, when the young woman was out of earshot. She hadn't offered to show her around or ask about special interests, merely put a pamphlet down on top of the membership card, sealed in plastic like a hymen. At least this girl was not as fierce as one I had joined recently who I thought was going to spit. She was standing beside her boyfriend too, and a complacent smile spread across his face. I thought of the A. D. Hope poem that compares brides to limousines . . . '*A sweet job! All she needs is juice! Built for a life-time . . .*': she had answered as though I had questioned her mileage.

'Sad, isn't it?' Mercy said, while I stacked one side of the trolley with Large Print and well-thumbed paperbacks, mainly romance. The young woman with the boyfriend in tow had headed resolutely towards the Romances, so the complacent smile was not justified. I could see her in a few years' time saying 'I keep myself to myself' and not lending anything on principle.

'We should have a bet on it. The next girl who comes along. The loser can buy lunch.'

'I'll take Miss then. I'm more self-controlled than you. Just the same, I'd like to hiss back at the next one.'

'And I'm going to kiss the next one who says Ms.'

There were still twenty minutes left before lunch. A young Taiwanese with an intelligent face and very swollen red hands asked for some UNESCO statistics; there were the usual requests for workshop manuals and a young woman who used to work in a pastrycook's asked for something to help her cope with her new baby. 'What do you do when you've got them home?' she said, as I took her upstairs to browse in 136.7. 'There's plenty written about before and having them, but not a lot about after.'

'Anyone?' I said to Mercy when I got back.

'No. There's not a likely person in sight.'

It was 12.50. I seized an armful of paperbacks and thrust them into vacancies on the revolving stand. *Passionate Vengeance, A Face in the Crowd, Doctor Deceived*, women enslaved by the lips of sheiks, exchanging vows above surgical masks, defeating men of experience with their innocence which called to a last, so infinitely frail, flickering innocence remaining. Rakes breaking down like low-burning coals in a domestic bedroom. I despaired for the province, for provincial girls, who, if they had heard of Ms, still saw no scenario to fit it in.

A young girl had approached the counter and I saw Mercy bend for the familiar pink registration form, open the drawer and select a white membership card and a plastic envelope. She peeled one membership sticker from the file and stuck it on the pink form and the other on the card below the line on which she would write the magic prefix. Doomed, I thought. The girl had a pale face like a violinist and fine straight conventional hair that might have been ironed. A girl who would be pleased to be called Miss, who might even be reflecting she would grow into it. The sort of girl you pitied, I thought, in spite of being talented; that a sheik or rake would ignore as they ignored the moon.

I could tell Mercy had left the question until last: 'Alexandra,' the girl said, blushing a little. 'Alexandra Mary Dodd.'

'It suits you,' Mercy said. 'Tall and stately.'

'I hate it,' the girl said. 'I'd rather be Alex.'

'Don't worry. My second name's Sybil.' She should be disqualified, I thought, for putting so much into it. I'd make up for it by shouting her lunch at the new cocktail bar that did enchiladas. No one should call me a poor winner.

'And how would you like to be addressed?' Mercy went on, turning her head for just a second and giving me a wink over a despairing eye. 'You're not Mrs?'

'I hope not,' said Alexandra Mary. 'At least not yet.'

'Would you like to be called Miss or Ms?' She said it so bluntly, so despairingly, I thought, that the girl must hear and be directed like a jury. Neutral, not savage. We could try the test again tomorrow and I'd buy her lunch anyway.

'I prefer Ms,' said Alexandra Mary Dodd.

Then she must have been thrown off guard by two librarians: one reaching across the counter to place a licked finger kiss on top of her hair, like a Sneetch delivering stars, and the other replacing a long black wand in its holder, and silently clapping the fingers of one hand against the palm of the other.

What Happened to the Pipers? ❧

I might have met them before but I remember them most clearly at a Royal Wedding party, where the women dressed as Barbara Cartland and the men in tuxedos. One of the women brought a tiny phial of honey pills and laid it beside her plate and Sabina wore her Calf Club medals fastened to her sash. Bob Piper was wearing a purple cummerbund which strained slightly at his middle and Susan Piper was in pale blue, hired from the Opera Company. I had only been invited at the last moment, since I was visiting the city to see my publisher: I half thought of converting my plain black dress to a maid. But there was more than enough jewellery in Sabina's drawers and the afternoon before, walking along the quays, I purchased a few yards of synthetic pink feathers to make a boa.

Just the same, I wasn't looking forward to it much. I'd been given a story to write on tugboats by an editor and I was already becoming slightly obsessed, inclined to bail people up and ask if the sight of two such close conspirators — they were very visible in the harbour, pulling ships in and out — wasn't thrilling. I even peered out the window of the house where the party was, hoping to catch a glimpse, when the hostess, whom I knew slightly, took our coats.

The moment our little party came into the room it was evident someone had taken pains. A long table like the spine of Queen Mary stretched the length of two rooms usually divided by double doors. On it a white cloth shone like ice and each place contained a card and a napkin folded into a crown. There were bowls of pink (what else?) roses and strategically placed, like timpani in an orchestra, champagne in silver buckets. And there were two television sets so that everyone, whatever side of the table they sat, could have a view of the crowds at the Abbey, the hats floating in like frisbees, the streets where there would be outbreaks of dancing, and the moments of apotheosis: the vague veiled shape of The Dress, which someone would describe, though only a tiny portion was visible, and the moment — the only one that moved me — when they broke through into the open air after the ceremony as though they had swum from the altar to the street.

'It will be a long night,' Bob Piper remarked and I thought he was referring to the programme, which the host was explaining would consist of many loyal toasts and a banquet number of courses. Bob Piper slid his hand inside his cummerbund with a wry expression and cast a half-alarmed, half-triumphant look at his wife. 'I don't suppose they eat everything,' she said, 'even at a banquet.'

'The Queen only drinks orange juice,' someone said, authoritatively.

'Ah, but I'm not a queen, am I, darling?'

We had drinks in the library first, the front room lined from floor to ceiling with books, and then we formed up in the passage and trooped in. There was even an additional male for me or I could have brought up the rear as a tweeny.

It settled down to being a long night. The ceremony itself was interminable, unless one was a royalist. I could tell the rapturous commentary was getting on Bob Piper's nerves. We drank to the Queen and the Calf Club medals; we drank to the Governor-General and then to the ladies who came into the Abbey. We drank to anyone we recognised: to Elton John, the King, occupying two chairs, of Tonga. We didn't drink to Nancy Reagan. 'Like butter on a hot skillet,' someone said. The lady certainly looked tense. So did Susan Piper, when Bob decided he'd be better off as a waiter and bent over someone's neck to bestow a kiss or flick a few drops of wine from his fingers down someone's cleavage. I saw her passing a warning look.

We were firmly divided into royalists and party types by the time the bride emerged from the Abbey. 'Why, her veil looks just like a wombat's tail,' someone said. Someone had had the foresight to position a camera in the tower and she drifted towards the light like a succulent morsel on the end of a ladle. The pillars of the Abbey were decked with greenery so it was like looking down a well.

'And here she comes into the light,' the voice was saying, 'veil into veil, only now the veil that was over her face when she entered is drawn back and she meets — just listen to it — the rapturous cries of her people.'

'Have you ever heard such waffle?' the red-haired man next to me said, as he declined the dessert — strawberries frosted with icing sugar — which was being passed on a tray.

'I expect they've lost all sense of grammar,' I said. 'It's natural to do that at a wedding.'

'And she said "Philip" instead of "Charles". Was that wish fulfilment? I've always thought Charles was rather wet.'

A heated argument began at one end of the table about Charles's tenderness to burnt children on hospital visits — someone had seen him lift a child swathed in bandages and clutching a small bear; he was infinitely pleasanter than Princess Anne. I saw Bob Piper put his head in his hands and groan and his wife kicked him under the table; they were sitting opposite — perhaps there is something in sitting side by side with your partner — eye contact, if it is not desired, can be painful. Shortly after he got up unsteadily and announced he was going to visit Herb.

I hadn't drunk very much that evening because I was going for a trip on the tugs: I desperately wanted not to be sick on board. I had just time to go back to Sabina's flat and change into warm clothes and flat shoes and be dropped at Queen's Wharf. I promised her I'd find my own way home and she drove off in her Calf Club medals, to get some sleep.

The harbour was choppy and I imagined the royal pair asleep, perhaps even chastely. Perhaps the prince was one of those rare, considerate lovers who allowed his bride a first night with simply their spines touching. One friend, newly divorced, had confided to me that that was the best part of a marriage.

The tugs too seemed married, the way they worked together: they reminded me a little of my parents: one preparing the meal and the other setting the table.

I stood on the flying bridge with the captain who had donned his braided coat and cap (regulations, he explained) and I thought he looked a little like a hero by Barbara Cartland. On the way back I discovered I was hungry and I ate with the crew in the galley, at a table groaning with fried eggs and bacon, tomatoes, sausages and bread.

*   *   *   *

I didn't see the Pipers or hear of them for a long time after that but one morning I found myself sharing a car with them. I had been out walking in the early morning and they pulled up near some traffic lights.

'We've just had breakfast with the sunrise,' Bob called out. 'Hop in and we'll take you wherever you are going.'

Susan told me she had had the idea of breakfasting in the Domain while the grass was still wet. 'We took a groundsheet, of course.' She had got the idea from a magazine.

' "One Hundred Ways to Save your Marriage", I guess it was,' Bob laughed. 'Drag your husband off for champers under a pine tree, sit him down on several pine cones.' Susan pinched his arm lightly, and they both laughed. 'Some of it was original,' she protested.

'Some of it was unique, darling.'

Love on a rug, I thought, and wished I wasn't so literal.

'Did you take champagne glasses?' I asked, to rid myself of a sudden ache due to pine needles.

'Yes. Plastic ones, of course. I bought them in Woolies on Friday night. Flutes, they are called.'

'And strawberry conserve. Fresh croissants. Curls of butter. Where the hell she got those.'

'From a restaurant, a chef I know.'

'A miraculous woman, full of surprises.'

I could practically see the article. 'Surprise Your Man: 101 ways to get the sap flowing.'

They had dropped me at the flat but didn't come in.

'We've had coffee,' Bob called.

'There might be another surprise at home.'

They roared off.

I revised my opinion after that and thought of the Pipers as a nearly perfect couple. True, Bob had threatened to undo his cummerbund and perform a bellydance in the dying stages of the Royal party, but I put it down to his reaction to royalty. I saw them — I was in the city for a few weeks on a course — at the opera, where they looked musical and absorbed in each other; they came by my friend's flat for coffee and could hardly keep their eyes off each other.

'Sometimes I find them a little bit stifling,' I said, aware of my envy, as we were drying glasses. There was a precious dinner service I was not allowed to touch, a Rosenthal. It was spread out on the dining table in piles: soup bowls, tureen, entrée plates. I thought Sabina had worked as hard as anyone married.

'I never envy apparent happiness,' Sabina said, taking a glass from my hand and redrying it. 'It always seems to take such work.'

'As much as this?' I asked.

'Oh, this is easy. The day's over for us, we can watch the soaps.' *Dallas* was on, followed by *Dynasty*.

She stood on a step ladder and I handed the precious plates up: she had cashed in her life insurance to pay for them on the grounds that fun now was better than money left to nieces and nephews. Then we sat on her long leather sofa, looking out at the harbour. In front of us, where the esplanade curved like the rim of a globe, was a small domestic patch of beach. And in the distance two familiar tugs, using a technique I could recognise — there was one on the shoulder and one braking — were working a large red container ship.

I went home, wrote the book on the tugs in a fever one weekend and didn't visit the city for nearly a year. When I did — I was in pursuit of a nautically minded illustrator — Sabina took me to lunch with Susan. We sat in a narrow booth in Molesworth Street, near Parliament, and there was hardly room at the table for our plates. Susan had a commodious calf-skin shoulder bag into which she burrowed for a tissue and said she felt a cold coming on. Her nose and ears looked pinched. Sabina had changed jobs and wore a smart new suit; they were discussing how far they had moved since the days when they were librarians together, wearing the faintly dowdy clothes, one up from writers, who were supposed to prefer shapeless lint-covered things.

'Sometimes it seems a lot simpler, just the same,' Susan said, and I thought she looked almost wistful. 'I remember I used to have lots of pendants and flat sensible shoes.'

They both agreed librarians had a certain way of moving, swinging through doors with shapeless skirts or leaning over a trolley as though pushing into the wind.

'Why is it, if we are so powerful now, we teeter on our feet?'

I thought smugly of my sandshoes when I went out on the tug and climbed down a ladder to the engine room backwards. I had imagined the tug might roll but, in spite of the fierce little chopping waves, it had seemed quite stable. Only outside the harbour was it vulnerable.

Susan's hands had chilblains but Sabina's were plump and soft and the nails were a new shade of vermilion.

Then, I must admit, the Pipers faded from my sight. My publisher moved and Sabina herself went on an extended trip. The city she lived in, which I swore was my favourite, was slowly replaced — I imagined it as a seduction, in which one's first denials are vehement that any possibility of attraction exists — by another. When Sabina returned she stayed in the same bay but moved further along. I introduced her to some new literary friends, who found her, as I expected they would, as enchanting as Elsa Maxwell. One memorable evening we staggered back to her flat from a Greek restaurant, four abreast, and I sprained my ankle in the gutter. Another time she left her purse on the roof of the car we were driving off in and it was tracked down to a nearby dairy. I, who knew of its discovery before the others, carried it back to her with the purposeful steps of a librarian getting off a public counter.

'How are the Pipers?' I asked from time to time, but my interest was desultory. After the picnic with the strawberry conserve and champagne I think I had settled into a residual envy. We strive for happiness and applaud the pursuit but expect the successful to look superstitious, as though they are perpetually touching wood. Sabina was bottling fruit and her normally crowded but ordered flat was full of jars steeping in footbaths: she had done gooseberries and gherkins and black truffle-coloured walnuts, where her mother had done peaches and tomatoes.

'Where are you going to put it all?' I asked in amazement, since already there was hardly room for the dinner service.

'I'll give some of it away for Christmas. Probably at least half.'

That was how we came to be heading the next day towards the Pipers' bach. It was a drive of nearly forty miles and seemed extravagant merely to deliver pickled walnuts, Sabina's special mango chutney and some cherries in brandy kept from the year before.

'You realise we'll probably come back equally laden and it won't solve anything,' I said, laughing.

'Susan might have a few fashion magazines or an old straw hat, but nothing more. The bach is very plain. Deliberately.'

Everything about them was deliberate, I thought. The deliberate breakfast in the Domain and now the bach, which I was already beginning to imagine: I saw two battered seagrass chairs bought from the mart before they became fashionable; a faded umbrella whose stripes had run; a windowsill decorated with shells. I was not far wrong. Except the chairs were plastic and there was a large faded canvas awning across the front, emphasising the look of a roadside stall.

We sat outside, the Pipers on the chairs and Sabina and I on rugs. The sea was not visible: the road dipped and another line of baches came between. But everything, as in a Mediterranean novel, was pervaded with it. The light was bleached and sharp, merciless to the corners of the eyes, and thin blades of kikuyu grass pushed through the peppery sand.

'How do you pass the time?' I asked. 'Besides the obvious.'

'Sleep until noon. Breakfast at midday. Generally we aim to follow Proust.'

I had noticed the twelve volumes, the first four slightly more worn, of *A la Recherche du Temps Perdu* in a little bookcase near a barometer.

'Eventually we'll only receive visitors in the middle of the night.'

'Two more weeks of bliss, darling,' Bob said, laying a hand on Susan's wrist. The back of his hand was covered with strong sparse dark hairs.

We went inside to collect the magazines and have a glass of lemonade. There were shells and sea-eggs on the windowsill and the sill was sandy. The floor was streaked with sand, an eternal invasion. Susan's figure was thicker in shorts than it appeared in the elegant dresses she usually wore: she had the beauty of an experienced Scandinavian movie star. A woman who travels at night to her lover, I thought, an unexpectedly passionate bourgeoise. Bob looked totally in his element: a seal with slightly rounded shoulders. He was one of those men with no discretion, whose animal spirits always worked with women.

'When are you coming again?' he said to Sabina.

'I thought I might try pickling onions.'

'I always wanted to marry a woman who could pickle onions. I'll divorce Susan and come away with you.'

'No thanks. I propose we meet once a year in a motel in a country town. We'll feast on pickled onions and not draw the blinds.'

'You're welcome to him,' Susan said. 'I'll pack his toothbrush.'

'Did I tell you she's given me an electric toothbrush? She must have had this weekend of ours in mind.'

The thought of onion eating and electric toothbrushing set me laughing and they had to hit me on the back when I swallowed some lemonade the wrong way.

'Look, her eyes are streaming. Are you sure she hasn't been into the onions?' Bob said.

But I could see Susan was not terribly amused. The room was too small and we had disturbed everything: the sand, the barometer, Proust, by intruding. Alone, Bob's hand would still have lain on her wrist and there would have been none of this badinage.

*　*　*　*

And that was the last I saw of the Pipers, *pipare* meaning to whistle. The tugboat book was published and enjoyed a moderate success: it was too local for its romance to spread. Sabina went steady and became domestic — not that she was not always that — and then went overseas. Her flat with its crowded luxury of pickled walnuts and Rosenthal dinner service was one of the reasons for visiting that city: we pretend it is our friends we come to see but it may be their houses.

She blew in from time to time from Chicago or New York and we caught up on news. She had become remarkably serious about her nieces and nephews.

One afternoon we were sitting on my verandah, drinking coffee and going, the way friends do, through a litany of friends. I thought some of our lives had become almost like short stories: not complete but enough had happened to pick an episode here and there. There were meetings I could begin in my mind, being met by Sabina, for instance, at the railway station and driving back to her flat in the bay, where the scent of preserves rushed out to meet us. 'I need a wife,' she had said that evening. 'The flat's a mess.' I thought it glowed against a phosphorescent sea.

So what happened to the Pipers?

'Still holding hands. Still at the beach? Susan wrapped in a loose sarong, a book with sand in its pages, Bob a dancing diving shadow at the wall?'

'Haven't you heard? Haven't I told you?' Sabina said. 'I'd no idea.'

'I'm the last person in the country to know anything,' I said. 'Even the end of my own marriage.'

'That's traditional. Don't blame yourself.'

'Thanks.'

I hadn't got tidier. That was one of my illusions. I too needed a wife.

'You know I always had a faint suspicion of something. There was something that didn't quite add up . . .'

She was enjoying telling the story, I thought: we always do when we have a preamble. I looked out over my garden, in which I had worked a little that morning: three white daisies stood out against a flourishing bed of honesty. I was only half listening. Wasn't it Schopenhauer who said that it takes an angel to rejoice in the happiness of a friend? Presuming, I always suspected, that one was unhappy at the time.

The Pipers, Sabina told me, had arrived with no papers.

She didn't mean they were illegal immigrants, just that their pasts, and there must have been pasts, were never spoken of. They were such a devoted couple, Bob so charming and Susan so complaisant, everyone took them at face value. They lived in breakfasts at the Domain, in intimate glances across dinner tables. Even their quick flaring spats were celebrated.

'People that live in the present convince us the past is not necessary,' Sabina was saying.

'Strictly they are correct,' I said, finding it an interesting idea. Sometimes I imagined the bench full of dishes that a late-night conscience had attended to.

Both Pipers — Piper was not their real name, they had chosen it from a telephone directory with a pin — were married to other partners. Both families in the small Canadian town they lived in were friends. They dined together and their children played together. Bob's wife was expecting their third child: they already had twins; her pregnancy may have made her myopic. Susan had two children to whom she was devoted and a charming if rather unsociable husband. They fled the country taking a single bag each and never communicated with their families again. They half hoped their spouses might marry and the families amalgamate. They had a solemn pact like people who have crossed each other's wrists in blood.

'You know a little of their lifestyle,' Sabina went on.

'Very little,' I protested. 'Why, I wasn't even paying attention. That lunch in the coffee bar with Susan.'

'Oh, Bob was notoriously unfaithful. It took Susan a while to find out. The inescapable logic of attracting such wholehearted sacrifice from her naturally drew other moths.'

'And she could never go back.'

'Nor could he. She must have represented his opposite.

Sensuousness with purity. I think he thought of her as a great candle. Like the Paschal candle in the church.'

'How did it end?' I asked. I didn't want to think back on Susan rubbing her eyes and complaining about people coughing in the office. Myself absolutely oblivious, like the twice-pregnant wife.

'In great style,' Sabina said. 'With almost the exact effect of the first departure. Not that he threw a party and hired a jazz band and caterers for supper then. He gave Susan the most tremendous fiftieth birthday party, two days of his most passionate loving at their bach, and then left in the dawn with a letter.'

Susan, it seemed, could not forgive Bob the manner of his going. They had been getting on so shakily before the party.

I imagined — since my own past was continuous, though I had often been tempted to interfere with it, at least it gave me leeway to imagine — that Susan had not showed for the party. I'd like to be able to say that was the day she pleaded a headache and went for a walk along the beach.

Excerpts from *A Journal of an Academic Year* 🐚

by Mary Cadwallader

Edited, with notes, by Felix Macdonald

A Journal of an Academic Year was found among the papers of Mary Cadwallader, deposited in the Fawcett Library, University College. Mary Cadwallader had indicated in letters to friends that a journal seemed an appropriate method of examining life in the university. In a letter to her long-time friend, Jessica Makepeace, dated before she took up her appointment, she noted with amusement that rumours of the projected journal were causing some consternation among faculty members. However it seems that the restraint she felt under — common to writers in the air of universities — communicated itself to her style and she was unable to complete the journal. The journal seems to have been written from a rough draft, since the handwriting is more than usually deliberate and well-formed. The cover of the journal is beige linen, closely covered with wild flowers in red, blue and gold. It measures 28cm x 22cm.

*   *   *   *

February 20th
Room 110

I am sitting on two volumes of the metropolitan telephone directory and wonder if I shall stay like this all year. The books, papers and half-open satchel of the young lecturer who had 110 before me are on a table against the wall. Also his timetable, growing weaker after August (the month he was taken away). Strangely I have just written the word *hospice* in a poem —

> *Breathing follows you to the gate*
> *And looking is something you must wear*
> *It is not quite time for the hospice*

('Leaving')

His field is semantics, which I am weakest at, but at his funeral two days later, one of his professors talks of his great love for the Scottish poets and I begin to feel at home. I wonder if I should volunteer for the English Dept choir, which performs at the service and is called The Throstles. To be anybody in this Dept one should really sing.

On my noticeboard I hang up my Stalin Writer's Medal — another elaborate joke from Jessica. It is a strip of wide blue ribbon with gold lettering and an Australian 20c piece spray-painted gold so the silhouette of the kangaroo stands out as though escaping from a bushfire.

After the funeral I walk under the trees, slowly back to 110, and get my manifold book. It is a year in which I should like, not to learn something about various sciences, since it is much too late for that, botany, zoology, and so on, but to project myself through imagination into their spheres. I think this idea originated when I was flying back from England. I was sitting next to a vet and we took turns at the window seat, not for the view but because you could rest your head. At one moment I looked out and was conscious that the stars had changed and we were in another hemisphere. It was like spinning a plate. I know nothing of stars, though I did once have a boyfriend with a telescope. My function was to keep it steady while he identified some planet; I hardly ever saw anything. But on this base of no or very minimal knowledge something, a memory perhaps, had stirred and I found it intriguing. Could a poem project itself with this no knowledge into the ether?

This morning there are cicadas under the trees — at least that is where the sound is. I dip my head under a tree on University Drive lawn and am reminded of a kind of ecstatic saw. A huge contrast between The Throstles and the cicadas. The Throstles have form and time and they finish things off, regretfully, like saying the white wine has run out — it is hardly ever red wine — but the cicadas have a manic quality like the death of Bhutto. It is like Pakistan stuck up a tree, thirty feet from the ground.

Professor Karlheinz Sturmer has very small feet. He handles words with great care and clarity. There is something about small feet that goes with precise brains.

I've been here nearly a month. My mention of Professor Sturmer's feet was an attempt at immediacy but already I've left it too late for that. Perhaps unwisely. But anything I wrote before this would have been like a shopping list. The strongest impressions which at the beginning are very like prejudices — Emma's prejudice against Mr Slope in *Barchester Towers*, for instance — are based on a kind of excess. So everything from now on, in this journal, will be modified. There will be no more mention of feet.

The hardest time at the university is arrival. I climb up

through Victoria Park, ignoring how many set pieces of art it resembles, and climb panting to my room. Open the door and then quietly close it behind me. Then I am not sure what to do. Is this the secret confession of all writers-in-residence? I look at my deskbook lying beside the typewriter. Yesterday's entry seems as far away as Kenya to the lions in the zoo. I can't remember thoughts I left with the evening before. It's a moment of panic like being body-searched at Heathrow airport. I usually flee downstairs and make a cup of tea (even Tennyson drank tea, I presume, and Wallace Stevens probably milkshakes.) There is the yellowing piles of *TLS* to go through and an article on 'Narcissism in the American Sex Life'.

> *Writing is better than not writing*
> *Slightly but not greater*
> *Than silence.*
>
> *Writing well is something to be aimed at*
> *Like a star through a telescope*
> *Through wind.*

Some *skunk* has stolen my coffee mug. I find this oddly cheering as though we really are studying Chaucer, Shakespeare and other giants. It is unwise to have too high an opinion of human nature, or if it rises up at times, it is always good to ground it on a little harmless pilfering. Mine *was* the best looking of all the mugs.

Cordelia and I follow part of the capping procession and see it cross the top of Montesquieu Drive before plunging downhill, like birds sliding off a branch. Before Cordelia arrives, I walk along the length of it on the other side of the road, like a Pharisee or an unaccredited journalist. My hands itch for a camera or a Mad Hatter's topper with 5/6d stuck in it. Obviously the highest echelons of the university are connected with birds — The Throstles, and now this. I remember the Norfolk pine in the school grounds, where the starlings left in graduation formation with nervous adrenalin-fixing shrieks and the well-wishes of the next rank. I sit (F.B.A.*) rather forlornly — it is rather a bleak day — near the underpass (to the Styx?) and write desultory verses in a notebook. From time to time a splendid vision appears on the path — a red scientist or a group of rabbit-soft B.A.s cluster for a photograph. One group throw up their caps, out of the frame. I wonder if the gowns walk the bodies inside them; I think of the old academics who led the procession, whose gowns and bodies match. Karlheinz offers me a twirl and puts on his bonnet (it looks like something from the French bakery) to show me. Later I get smuggled into the Chancellor's bunfight. It's exactly like being surrounded by life-sized birds, wondering if I'll get pecked.

A Winter Programme of Lectures

Professor Barbour will speak on lyric/antilyric
Lamb on Derrida, Richardson and Montaigne.
For the prosaic, The Interpretation of Ruins
And into our hands, Words and Contemporary Art.

*Failed B.A. Commonly used in India for a candidate who sits but fails to attain a degree. Mary Cadwallader had part of a degree.

> *The Grief of Teutonic Women: Alas and wei la wei*
> *And The Eyrbyggja Sagas, their Feminine Characters*
> *Will be leavened by Robert Lowell*
> *And The Coming of Death in Morality Plays.*

> *The season of fitfulness combines with fires*
> *And fossils speak in departmental seminars*
> *They are pieces of ruins but each is complete*
> *Like an ash wall with some lids ajar.*

And I have a nameplate:

> *A name, a name*
> *No wonder Richard called for*
> *A horse, a horse*
> *At least it had four feet.*

I receive a letter from Kenneth Wales beginning: 'Since I've always thought of you as a fine young chap, an automatic selection for the First Eleven, one of the golden-haired boys and an example to all men, I find no difficulty in thinking of you as a Fellow of a University.' Cheering words, even if the sex is wrong, and a proper recipe for demeanour. What if the brain in the skull is not academic though? I just hope my invisible tiger coat with First Fifteen stripes hides it. Or maybe I'm just a bit of a bounder. Rilke is kinder when he says: 'there is too much opposition in my nature to their kind' (he means universities). There is no opposition at all in mine but a kind of incompetence which the shortest period has revealed, confirmed, sealed and delivered as though I have already graduated. F.B.A., the dark nucleus in the centre of gowns, like a man tied on to a horse or under a sheep's belly. I console myself, walking into the university by the tradesmen's entrance, by thinking of Julian Huxley and his mother's quicksilver flashes of images, which often ran too fast for her to express and which the great scientist retained a liking for, in fact thought them the best of his heritage. The feeling of being a fraud — an easily cornered one, for all that — is overcome by a feeling of glee.

Here to prove my thesis and endless carelessness is the title of a lecture by a visiting professor: 'Glottal Stop in Tahitian French: a Reflection of Historical and Contemporary Bilingualism'. I shan't go because it sounds horribly like choking.

Cordelia and I on the way to lunch go past, nearly fall into, a hole in the path near the Geography Dept. (Geographers seem rather untidy types, though my survey is rather sporadic.) One of the diggers asks: 'Are you the two young ladies who are looking for bones?' When we look puzzled, he continues: 'Do you have wet-weather gear?' I think we are expected to get into the hole. Cordelia reassures him and we line up for stew (today it's called goulash) — at least I have that and Cordelia has a green apple which goes beautifully with her pale skin and pale blonde hair. The peel, as it comes off the apple, the underside of it, is the perfect touch of a great artist. But I am disappointed about the hole. Another chance missed. Who knows where we would have come out?

Not only am I not an academic, as Rilke felt he was not, but I am aware now, often painfully, of the penumbras that the knowledge carries around with it. I cross lightheartedly enough across some of these invisible barriers and find myself floundering like a very clumsy dragon. I am the wrong size for the scenery, my attempts at jokes (and also to cover up) have the wrong terminology, I say the clumsy obvious thing and then cannot elaborate it. I listen to the language and it seems to have changed — some sentences could surely be cut or the message they are carrying is actually quite simple — I hardly dare offer 'Do you mean . . .?' I sit at the table like a giant bird blown off course among dainty deadly creatures (I mean their brains) and try to adjust to their size of titbit. I know if they were to fly away together, or form a cluster, a medieval city might appear or 'The Female Characters of the Eyrbyggja Sagas'. In a sense there is no new ground, nothing for my rough beak to get into. Any theory I have is quite outsize and not very coherent. There was a bird like this on television recently. It was so large it was being weighed in a plastic clothes basket. It feebly pecked at the hand of the scientist who approached it, with a great beak that clapped together. I wouldn't be surprised to learn that its nest hadn't been made for it; it looked uncommonly like packing straw.

My departmental seminar was rather feeble. The politeness of the audience was a little inhibiting. I was very grateful for Felix Macdonald for sometimes giggling very softly. I find it so odd being looked at with any kind of respect; it immediately brings out a kind of levity. The worst part was failing abysmally to answer a tripartite kind of question from a young woman with her hair scooped back — I'm sure I didn't even answer one part of it — before I was totally lost. Partly it was nervousness plus delivery followed speedily by exhaustion, and partly because my brain doesn't seem to work in straight lines. If I catch sight of her at any time in the corridor, I shall apologise.

Four months have gone and the university seems almost

familiar. First of all it was a bit like becoming a Catholic and being morbidly afraid of religious statues — in this case the statues were minds. Now I regard them with a certain shrewdness, in which a part of envy remains, but not too much, as it was at the beginning. At the beginning I was inclined to be defensive and rationalise: the academic mind seemed to emphasise my carelessness, which I suppose, if I am honest, I defended, thinking it had something spirited in it, like a photograph in this evening's paper of a horse making a mess of leaping a hedge, so rider and horse are both flying in unlikely shapes towards a nose landing. Of course this is not spirit: simply a kind of illogic in the legs. Wilfully jumping from one inaccurate conclusion to another, as I do, is not a virtue, but I see with amusement the virtue I am excusing and admiring is under this, even under the spectacular fall and the jockey with the broken ribs. I feel the attitude has something right in it (for me), though it hardly ever produces the results that would convince anyone else. Settling this, even partially, has made my admiration for the academic world greater. They lack this foolishness and deserve commendation for it but I long to race alongside them like a horse in a field against a train. Of course the horse very soon reaches the boundaries of his field (open field is such a nonsense) and has to go sideways where the train goes on. The horse follows the hedge or goes into a corner and kicks its heels.

I am sitting at the edge of the tunnel on a wooden seat warmed by a sun with enough heat in it to offer a contrast with the wind. Eventually the cold will be overthrown and it will be summer. But I shan't be here for the hot sticky months which I would like to try again. It is the same place I sat in watching the academic gowns alight on the lawn like so many birds. I've become so used to going through the tunnel, on the way to lunch, on the way back, it's like going through a watch. Why do years have to end before you get used to them? Why can't I play this one again?

'In order to do something one must *be* someone', Goethe wrote. I am thinking of this coming through the tunnel this morning. Most artists I have met would take the cake for cunning. One was lecturing to a crowd of students on the Arts and Commerce overpass this morning — they were strung out alongside him with sketch pads with drawings of the quad. Later the pads were propped up against the wall as along the banks of the Seine and the students passed up and down while he called out comments. The sun here of course makes everyone screw up their eyes — so much so it has become an art theory of itself. What the students seemed to be after — comparing his infinitely more screwed-up profile with their own blank ones — is the shrewdest look, the laser eye in a goatish face. This is surely not what Goethe was after. I suppose art is always a kind of growth and from time to time the parts in the rear need attending to. Rather like the mother of Gigi in Colette, who with a small amount of water still made a careful toilette before sleeping.

Academic minds come in sizes and strengths. There are orthodox ones whose opinions I trust implicitly — they never send out distress flares or have men overboard. Others are ornate, like fine embroidery; they take a year in a writer's life and in their analysis and love and concentration forget he was ever bored or fragile, like the Impressionists — they remind me of someone in a Casualty Dept bandaging the toe of a man involved in a serious accident. Others take a big topic — Sterne, for instance, or Dickens — and swell outwards like an overflowing bath. There are medievalists who are still afraid of death, geologists of rock falls, philosophers of not getting a rebuttal right. The luminaries have it both ways: an early consolidation (probably several summers' reading) and then a leap from a toehold. A bit like Goethe, they are aiming to be and do.

The main problem with journals is their silliness?

Clarence Villiers has written seven poems, now eight in one day. I tell him he should be put down. The prodigal was really prolific, I think, and this is why he was able to return to his room. In fact I wonder if prodigal and prolific are not confused. Or did the Father secretly recognise it? The brother was certainly only pragmatic, given to inspecting pig sties. To be prodigal means a sabbatical and writing a journal. How often you hear a wistful note in people who fed a gas meter with their last shilling or spent all day in bed (with pigs) to keep warm. Of course they don't want the experiences again, there is no sign the prodigal went back for fresh material, but there is a piquancy about it nonetheless. The English Dept is planning an end-of-year farewell to Professor Forrester-Greene — three pigs' heads among other delights. I pass Cordelia on the path and she talks of a triad.

'Visceral', Clarence says, is where most poetry begins — 'intestine, liver, lungs and other internal organs of the body'. It is these that this year is supposed to be maintaining, changing the fluid around, giving a spring clean. Sometimes I feel like an economic advisor — the results are years away. Except perhaps economic advisors do not have the guilt of their own projections. One million words have failed to find employment, they are disheartened; some are talking of joining the army. There they will learn to fix clauses, not split infinitives, they will rush about with spanners assembling the general's speeches. The part of you that lives, Clarence was implying, and it sounded swampy like the mangroves at the edge of Palliser Bay. What has not cooled, or solidified, what has not been dealt with, so it is like dried dung. Something from the air reaching down, depth calling to depth. It's a large order when my brain feels spongy, no clear city, or space galaxy, but a visceral suburb.

Boxes and bundles of exam scripts replace the autumn leaves: symbols hold and decline. How odd it is to think we master them. If they go off anywhere it is like one of those tricks at the microphone: circle of pattering feet getting fainter and fainter, voice calling a fading reprise. Perhaps each person just gets so many.

The boxes pass up and down and the brains rest in the sun, under trees, in postures of nonchalance or tension. Another box goes past, carried with the resoluteness of a beefeater. Perhaps I should spring out from behind a bush and stage a hold-up. Aegrotat passes all round, like my Latin teacher who eternally begrudged the sinking of the ship carrying her master's papers to England. There were no honours that year, and perhaps harder to bear, no failures.

I no longer pause so much at the door to my room: that first morning start has gone. This must be what it is like to be an old professor. How strange that it has taken me up to the last term to feel truly at home. I've spent some days reading as well: solid reading, I suppose you could call it, if the term wasn't so intrinsically impossible. I guess solid is intended for the results. Now I wonder whether the long poem I am writing will affect the shorter poems. I try one or two and they have changed a little, a bit like a horse at the Technology Museum I had a ride behind, in a gig. It was a pacer and wanted to pull.

Dear Albatross — that's the way one should address a journal.

Dear bloody Albatross. How far behind I am, as though I've spent the whole year in Room 110, dreaming. What's the use of trying to write *and* digesting. Digesting comes first and notes. But not real writing. And when the first impressions are gone? The first impression of the Senior Common Room, for instance, where at the beginning I leaned my elbows on the table and looked out at the huge (over-huge, too huge for Constable to make any use of them) sedate trees in Pompallier House garden and kicked myself surreptitiously on the ankle for pleasure. Then it was like being surrounded by dons, or at least Ph.D.s. Now it's almost a commonplace, or am I pretending? Through the tunnel and out, through the gardens and out, and lunch. Ploughpersons. Even the menu is predictable. The very nice way they have with lasagne, in a creamy sauce. The chili con carne: more doubtful. Never quite having the nerve to try a pie. Eschewing the soup which seems vaguer than its titles. And The Buttery. Wasn't that a case of falling in love with a word?

From the Zoology Dept, above the porch and against a small window, is leaning a chute constructed of boxes, looking for all the world like an elephant's trunk. Where the elephant's foot has gone is another matter. I should like to see it again, my favourite thing in the museum. I imagine it on the dining-room table, filled with some incongruous food. The inside would have to be treated of course. An archaeologists' dinner party. 'Pass the elephant's foot, will you, Clive.' It wouldn't be the least out of place.

Regarding the Zoology Dept from outside

One whole elephant would account for
The architecture: a five-roomed house
With upper sleeping quarters: a mini-Tatler
Place for elephant and spouse.

Inside of course there are only relics.
The hunters have been here before us:
One elephant's foot complete with toenails
A bit of tusk and other etceteras.

Apart from that files, filing cabinets.
One professor with an upside-down flamingo
In a glass bottle like a long-lasting rose.
Elephant memorial, I suppose.

Eclipse of the moon. Forrester-Greene looks through a bus ticket and its six variegated clips are turned into six small nearly new moon reflections on the ramp to Level 4. A small cluster of us stand around, a sort of paper Stonehenge. I go over to the bank and another group (scientists no doubt, or botanists) are clustered, grinning sheepishly, around the reflection of a palm tree. Small clusters of brains, I think, going back to the underpass. And these small clusters seem almost enough.

Lunch with Villiers and Vassella in the University Club. The two Vs. Vallender is away. The three horsemen of the V. Actually this department is strong on V for some reason. We have an elegant lunch of smoked rabbit, avocado and smoked salmon. We talk (the Vs mainly and I listen) about birds (including several bird imitations, descriptions of quails' tails and habits and so on) and salmon fishing. A little about politics and the 1918 influenza epidemic. On the way back through Pompallier House gardens, between the two distinguished Vs, Villiers breaks into melodious Middle French and Vassella translates. I feel immensely privileged, immensely happy.

*   *   *   *

Though the journal ends on a note of 'happiness' (the last entry), it was abandoned at that point. The emphasis on birds throughout is worth mentioning, perhaps as intimations of flight, or the wish to escape the tedium of entries. The journal is little more than half full (81 out of 156 pages). Mary Cadwallader has written of 'the fire of first drafts'; she must have been aware of the irony of abandoning it.

Nights at the Embassy ❧

It is Rosamunde's fault that we are to read at the Embassy: in her unfailing friendship she has phoned and asked the social secretary if I can be included. I am eating a boiled egg at her dining table when she phones and I try to hold up a napkin in protest.

'All fixed,' she says, rejoining me. 'Just a few poems, followed by the guest speaker. The ambassador will conduct proceedings.'

Then, quite calmly, as though the day has not been ruined, she goes on spreading avocado on triangles of toast and airily applying black pepper.

'I know I shall mention pork or Arabs,' I say to Rosamunde as we join the throng approaching the Embassy door.

'There won't be pork,' she says firmly. 'Or Arabs.'

The house is deceptively ordinary behind a high fence. The garden is beautifully, if recently, planted with low non-concealing shrubs. There are a prodigal number of lanterns.

It is inside, in the arrangement of its rooms and offices, that the house differs. For it seems it has no bedrooms: it is a house simply for functions. Hall spills into reception area and the reception area is expandable, like a priest's house. Discreet screens allow for a smaller, more intimate party. The decor is light and pleasing and the quantity of flowers stupendous. And so warmly are we received that no one thinks of a duty evening gown or getting into the soup and fish.

'I suppose they say gefillte fish. Getting into the soup and gefillte fish,' I say nervously, thinking of Bertie Wooster.

Having been relieved of our coats and invited to freshen up, we are eyeing ourselves in mirrors in a small dressing room.

'I don't know what you are talking about.'

'What shall we do with our books? Carry them under our armpits?' Later I must tell Rosamunde that this is where the Vikings kept their money, secured with beeswax. I presume it was to leave their hands free for fighting.

'Carry them like a clutch purse.'

'What are you going to read?'

'I thought the ones about my granddaughter. And you?'

'The Vikings. And something else.'

A single Viking sock had been discovered and this was thought to undermine a scenario of wildly pealing church bells, rapine and smoke. At the end of a sea-coloured skein of wool a Viking woman — they were reputedly fiercer than the men, who were regarded as 'big softies' — sat knitting a sock which she stretched from time to time to estimate the length of her horned one's foot. Somehow this had become entangled with the vision of Miss Marple in fluffy wool, plotting mischief.

The ambassador has placed a small table with a lace cloth for us to sit behind as we are introduced. Then, with our books in our hands, we are expected to read for no more than five minutes. The visiting writer will be called on to thank us and say a few words about the purpose of her journey and her general impressions.

'I shall say that the water truly does go down the plughole in an anticlockwise direction,' she says with a laugh when we are sitting together. 'I checked it this morning. My sons are longing to know if it is correct.'

I think of the world spinning with all the handbasins and baths of one hemisphere upside down, clinging grimly on, held by a suction like a tattoo. And on the other hemisphere the basins are the right way up and perfectly unconscious of anything unusual.

Sascha, my sister-in-law, had dragged me through the entrance of the Jorvik Centre and before I could protest, a motorised car and a commentary was pulling us backwards through the Great War, the Boer War, Florence Nightingale, Cavaliers . . . into the cacophony of Viking village life. An awesome amount of grunting, mumbling, clinking, hammering, wassailing broke out, with under foot the motifs of screeching cats, hens on the wing, dogs masticating bones. To underline this eternity, a Viking crouched on a latrine surrounded by stakes, straining to move his bowels. Long before we passed him and skirted the vast barn in which a Viking orgy and eisteddfod was in progress, I had decided I hated the Vikings.

Rosamunde and I are very different, so different that I am often amazed. We point in the same direction, like beagles, we have the same sense of smell, love of the chase. But we are amazingly different in our prefaces. Once when we were travelling together, this difference revealed itself around two telephone calls.

The lights in the hotel we were staying at had fused and we had stumbled across the road and over a ditch to a solitary telephone box where we struck matches and fumbled for coins. One of us was carrying a large bottle of brandy.

We were phoning our daughters at university, who were sitting exams. But Rosamunde's conversation owed nothing to the night or the occasional apocryphal lights from passing trucks: it was orderly and discreet as if she was phoning from the Ritz.

When my turn came, I devoted it almost entirely to a description of the night, of disorder, the danger of the ditch outside. I was so concerned with setting the scene that I almost forgot the examination.

'The Vikings Wore Socks' is not a good choice for the Embassy.

> *Someone has found one*
> *Which somehow disgusts*
> *Viking marauders*
> *Their feet cased in socks*

Am I suggesting the Israeli army is over-equipped? The ambassador, with his arms folded on his abdomen, looks bemused. As we are circling the buffet, I overhear him explaining that he is a major in the army, as well as an ambassador. 'And my wife outranks me. She is a lieutenant-colonel.' This information seems to give him a great deal of pleasure and I wonder, for a moment, if the serious-faced waiters are in the army as well.

There is one woman I feel drawn to that night because her elegance is so careless: she exudes danger and, I think, the capacity to handle her own fire power, like Lauren Bacall. It is she who draws from me the word 'pig' and adds 'Arab' a second later.

We are being shepherded towards second helpings at the buffet and I demur, without thinking: 'I'll be as fat as a pig.' The Lauren Bacall woman rocks on her heels with delight, claps me on the shoulder. 'What a wonderful fox's paw, my dear,' and sinks to the floor with a loaded plate. 'I'll just squat here, like an Arab.'

I think of her, and try to avoid her eye, as I go on doggedly:

> True the ocean is cold
> And they came a long way
> And their wives had long evenings
> Free from looting and rape

It seems I have committed a messianic error of taste.
There is no mention of pork but looting and rape are not
suitable accompaniments to rumtopf and Ugat Schekademe.
The editors, near the fireplace, are doing their best to look
like bankers. When I come to the last verse I almost feel the
harsh Viking wool rubbing against a blister.

> And a man and a sock
> Both long dead of course
> Does a tiny bit unravel
> The woolstrings of the heart.

I look up at a circle of non-committal faces and see
Lauren Bacall clap with two fingers on her palm, like knitting
needles.

Rosamunde, who never forgets what is due to her listeners
— hadn't she spoken first to her daughter's flatmate, allotting
him time and respect, while I fed the coins in and felt like
pacing? — has remembered, before she reads, to thank the
ambassador for both our invitations. She turns towards the
honoured guest and says 'Haere mai' three times, like Black
Rod, while I quail inwardly, aware I have been thinking
only of a first line. How grateful I am to hide under this
greeting, to begin with 'Like Rosamunde . . .'

Then she reads two poems about her granddaughter,
personal poems that even in that replete and restrained
circle bring a murmur of appreciation, and one about a
collection of marble eggs she keeps in a bowl by her gas fire.

I read something about a sputnik and a magnolia tree and we sit down to polite applause. Then the guest speaker gets up and talks about the quantity of grass and sheep, the need for entente, and how the water goes down the plughole.

There had been another room at Jorvik which I have tried to forget. A room so potent I could have turned back to the straining Viking with a Hail fellow, Well met. It was in the section where the commentary was almost exhausted, where it moved into our own century, with its white coats and laboratory benches.

It was nothing but compacted mud really, with tiny sticks like tapers showing through. In a few seconds we would reach the spot where the Coppergate Helmet was discovered and the time car stop. But here, with the sticks like rows of worn-down teeth, was the level at which the Vikings had lived. Tons of human and animal excrement had been removed, sacks of teeth, bins of shards, caches of jewellery and flints, and this, in spite or really because of our man behind the arras, was all that remained. Life, loot and socks gone in this fearsome pity in which the sticks were upended birds' feet, signalling.

The evening at the Embassy does not last long after the speeches, though we are cordially pressed to linger. In the vestibule, while our coats are being brought, there is a move to master one word of Hebrew.

'*Lie*-la-tov,' we try tentatively and then, bolder, call it in little groups into the night. The lawns, with their efficient sprinklers, are doubly drenched with dew. The moon is a huge denarius. '*Lie*-la-tov.' Between a sweet and a missile. '*Lie*-la-tov.' Then someone points out a falling star and the evening and the star is gone.

'One of the waiters had a shoulder holster under his dinner jacket. I caught a glimpse,' Rosamunde's husband says when the last '*Lie*-la-tov' has died and we are walking alongside the high fence.

'I wonder if it was the one I asked for a glass of water? I thought he looked rather surprised.'

'I expect he is not used to being a waiter.'

'I told you I would say "pig",' I say and, now we are out of earshot, I start giggling. Rosamunde joins in and soon we cannot stop and our sides are aching.

The next morning we will write thank-you letters, with slightly different phrases and endings. Rosamunde's ends: 'With sincere appreciation' but mine is simply 'Yours sincerely'.

I imagine the Embassy door is closed now and the Lauren Bacall woman has taken off her shoes and is dancing with the gunman. He has loosened his tie and his jacket is flung over a chair. The ambassador is smoking a cigar and the honoured guest is testing her theory once again and taking a bath. Or putting through a long distance call to Tel Aviv where her husband lectures at the university.

I imagine a sense of relief is sweeping over them, has swept over them from the second the door closed and the gunman surveyed the front porch and part of the gravel driveway through the peephole.

Lauren Bacall reclines against the gunman now, arms loosely around his neck. The wave of her hair swings against his cheek as she murmurs in his ear 'That frightful woman who said "pig".'

Wie Geht's? ❧

St Fructuosus of Tarragona

Beatrix,

Wie geht's?

What will happen if we chose the same St Fruit on the same day? Will there be a small explosion? A burst bag of oranges or two damson plums fermenting together inside brown paper? And did you know *Wie geht's* is a vulgarity: it says so in a thriller I am reading. '*Wie geht's* is not elegant German. It has become an Americanism, like chop suey.'

But how can it matter if letters are vulgar or careless? They are not intended to be kept. It's part of the pact that they should rush upon their subject matter with the same impulse that set Elizabeth Bennet crossing field after field and getting her petticoat in a disturbing state. How else could the next scene have been written? Without the mud there could have been no turns on the carpet with Miss Bingley, when both their figures were adjudged equal. I can almost hear Miss Bingley hiss under her breath 'I've taken off the martyrish petticoat. Now let's see how she does against my walk, my waist.'

We are both engaged in occupations of such precision: you scrawling algebra across a blackboard at St Hilda's and me in a laboratory with an experiment that has been going on far too long.

The saints' names are a reminder of our Catholic schooldays. I am curious to know who you are going to use next. St Fructuosus reminds me of those little sachets of sherbert with a licorice straw to suck through. Today it would be cocaine. Wasn't there something suggestive about the way the corners of the sachet were folded and stapled? After a day in this forsaken laboratory I could easily lay my nose alongside a trail of cocaine. None of my figures compute, but still the experiment bubbles merrily away. My trouble is I was reared on Marie Curie and imagined myself working with pitchblende.

I've just measured my forehead with the callipers: I'm sure it is nothing compared to Marie Curie's. I think of her as a street lamp, burning remorselessly.

It's after midnight so St Fructuosus has had his day.

Alice

St Katherine dei Ricci

Beatrix,

Wie geht's?

In a little butcher shop across from my flat — a shop with a green-and-pink striped awning, which is new — they are selling white veal. It is evidently the latest thing to have at dinner parties. The shop seems extra dark — or am I imagining it? — and the sawdust on the floor by the chopping block is so clean it is a wonder it is not sold as well. The butcher, who wears a little boater with a ribbon to match the awning, explained it is to do with diet and lack of sunlight. At least that is what I think he said. His own face is as pale and pinkly healthy as a pig's head.

I had a dinner party recently in which I rendered myself redundant. I chose the most complicated recipes and had to keep scurrying back to the kitchen. At one stage I found myself with the door closed between kitchen and dining room and addressing an enormous pile of plates that had had green soup in them. I had obviously had one too many drinks. I opened the door a crack and the conversation was so animated I thought of not returning at all. Do you wonder that my secret desire is to be one of those old ladies who live on the top floor of hotels with their meals flying up to them in the dumb waiter.

When everyone had left I drank the dregs of all the glasses and did the dishes listening to *La Forza del Destino*.

I had prepared some subjects in my head in case the conversation flagged but it proved unnecessary. Do you want to know what they were? Don't laugh.

1: Does anyone remember the Dreyfus case? I'd so like to have it explained to me.

2. Is anyone else so influenced by food in books?

Luckily these options were not taken up.

Alice

The Forty Martyrs

Beatrix,

Wie geht's?

If I hadn't been so obtuse I would have noticed how frequently hints have been appearing about the gym instructor. Then I look at the top of this page and see the Forty Martyrs and wonder if they were not ambushed. You say you discovered him one lunch hour with a book, a very serious book, and this is a good sign. You don't mention the name of the book so I have no way of judging. Was it *Emma*, for instance, or something by Kierkegaard? But I admit you were right to cast a look at the spine: skills on the parallel bars hardly count for much if there is no brain. Perhaps you could tell me the title next time you write and I can go on with my analysis.

I am beginning to doubt analysis: in my business it would be so easy to move a decimal point or doctor a column of temperatures. It is wrong to think of analysis leading anywhere, which is the hope one has at the start. Instead it is like the *London A-Z*: tiny streets, like crystals, thicken in an area no bigger than a fingernail until one practically sees the life in them: the households, the dining tables, the gas metres. If you are attempting to analyse anything in this pursuit (your word), don't.

I wonder about the Forty Martyrs though, if there wasn't something faulty in their reasoning. They seem to have been affected by a common impulse, a group decision. How much of love is a group decision it is hard to say.

Alice

St Euphrasia Pelletier

Beatrix,

Wie geht's?

I was seriously tempted by St Waudru, who sounds like a walrus, but Pelletier sounds like stitching, needlepoint, ecclesiastical embroidery in white silk. What you are engaged on — though your last letter is rather evasive — reminds me of sewing or rather weaving. The parallel bars are a kind of weft and your algebraic formulae sit on them like notes on a stave.

'It is serious, I think,' you said and the title of the book was *The Magic Mountain*. You say he likes books about the whole life, *Bildungsromane*. That at least shows a longing for completion.

I don't see, myself, why we should not make slight efforts to turn our lives into novels. I mean, instead of queuing to see queens and princes pass in open landaux by holding periscopes up to our eyes, we should deliberately invest in some ceremonies of our own. Of course we shan't totally succeed but there are walks in cemeteries, meals on houseboats, slow peregrinations to sections of the museum.

I've taken to walking, while my experiment boils and bubbles, in the old cemetery opposite. Its few graves have a great deal of space between them — no chance here of Galway Kinnell's lascivious bones — and quite a few of them lean like pre-braces teeth. The tiny church has some kind of preservation order and is only opened for the occasional wedding.

This sets me to thinking of you and what progress you are making. You say you are determined not to be a plotter and then find your feet tending along a path where he will be sitting, still engaged on *The Magic Mountain*. The danger of such books is they come to a dead halt: you must somehow distract him.

I recall you were not very athletic at school. I can remember playing tennis with you, using, by tacit agreement, only forehand shots. Do you remember the gym mistress passing and turning her head away in despair, even making a continental gesture with her hands? When I think of this I wonder if the whole thing is ill-advised. But then, as you sensibly say, a man who spends his working hours in callisthenics may want a life that is more restful than other men. Let us hope you are right.

Alice

St John of Nepomuk

Beatrix,

Wie geht's?

Well, the churchyard and the walks have come to an end and I'm bent over the test tubes and my columns of figures. It may be that no one wants to know how mangroves reproduce but my professor wants some kind of result by the end of the year. Even negativity must be weighed like so many pounds of flesh. I protested that there might be a breakthrough but he talked of parameters and then — it seems I had caught him in a good mood because he has been invited to a distinguished conference — he went on about science being like casting a net over the Milky Way. I felt as though I had been sprinkled, like Wendy, with stardust from Peter Pan.

Don't apologise for saying very little up until now: love's like science in that respect: say too much, read too much into it, and it evaporates. Now you've come clean and listed: a dinner, a walk around the hockey field late one afternoon (mercifully fewer girls about to see you, though you *will* have been seen) and now an invitation to a play. I hope you will confess in plenty of time that you do not swim and haven't mastered the backhand return. Do this early and it will be seen as charming.

One of my boyfriends was very annoyed when he found out I couldn't snorkel. I suppose this man of yours is very *physically* attractive.

Alice

Sts Gervase and Protase

Beatrix,

Wie geht's?

A photo no less. And in colour. You say you are not sure about the focus but I can see he's in good shape. The way he stands on the stones — I'm sure he could easily cross a river on boulders — and his chest seems rather deep, like a good set of drawers. If only you were in the photo I could tell more. You say he has finished Thomas Mann — he reads one author at a time — and is going on to John Masters. If he is at the Ms now he must have begun when he was in short socks. I'm glad you've told him about our games of tennis but a little alarmed that he has offered to coach you this summer. Did you explain that forehand only makes for quite a lot of excitement, with swift crab-like dashes to the side? We had some amazingly good rallies.

It is kind of you to ask about my work. The professor has relapsed into a more normal mood and exchanges curt greetings when I encounter him in the corridor. This signifies he has given me an ultimatum. So much for imagining myself a Curie. When you think of it, what an adoring light Pierre must have cast on her.

Do you think it is wise to change your diet? A gymnast might require red meat but do you need it for algebra? I know Marie Curie was restored by *un bifteck et pommes de terre frites* but that was when her blood sugar was very low. You might be compelled to burn it off in games of tennis. I recommend nothing more strenuous than croquet. It seems to go with algebra.

Alice

St Antony of the Caves

Beatrix,

Wie geht's?

You say you are eating steak twice a week and have had your first game of tennis. You were defeated, naturally, but you managed a backhand drive which was out but ran along the tramlines. You were expecting something far worse.

I have begun tabulating my results and hope to write a paper. Perhaps this accumulated negativity will prevent someone else from going down the same desiccated path. When you look at it this way, lack of success can be ground covered. It is impossible to speed every mile with Bach on the stereo.

I don't know how we are to manage these dark unilluminated patches in our lives except, as I think I said before, with some bright private ceremony. Sometimes in a maidenly kind of English novel a cup of tea at a Lyons Corner House seems to fit the bill.

Have you an algebraic equation that takes in this man you are modelling your life on? $X + Y$, which would include not only the tennis and the steaks but the possibility of X's house or Y's and what is to be done with the surplus furniture.

You say you are not nearly as advanced as that: that these domestic hints are like the sudden scent of a flowering bush, so potent when you come on it, but in such a lot of plain air. Who can tell how many other algebra mistresses have tried underdone meat and had their tennis game improved?

You hinted I was behaving like Mrs Bennet in her dressing room, counting her unmarried daughters on her fingers and trying to find out what the suitors ate. In that case I wish you carriages and a house on an eminence and a park and a phaeton to go round it.

Alice

St Elizabeth Bichier des Âges

Beatrix,

Wie geht's?

You were offended by my last letter and I don't blame you. I often let my imagination run away with me. One absurdity creates another. I didn't mean to imply you were cohabiting or even about to cohabit. I was simply trying to look into the future when all these decisions: your twice-weekly game of tennis at the club and your table at the Beefeaters' Arms have settled into a routine. Isn't, as someone said, a routine just a name for something we do twice?

My own work is so painstaking I want to scream. My supervisor — the professor is now overseas — seems more particular about non-results than he would be about splitting the atom. It is not enough that no one needs to cross this field again but each mine must be mapped and then we must go into how much explosive and the position of a clump of daisies. He admits I am unlikely to advance because of it and should think of changing my direction next year. I think someone else wants this room. To console me, and on the professor's recommendation, he is putting my name forward for a conference in London.

You know I am terribly afraid of the word 'subsume'. It seems to have such a terrible sucking sound to it, a vicious sloping edge where the sea bites at a throat of sand, where everything seems hurried up. Not the slow wearing down of boulder to pebble to grain. I believe that might have been behind the frivolity in my last letter. Apologies.

Alice

St Cloud

Beatrix,

Wie geht's?

I felt compelled to look up St Cloud and find he was a prince who renounced a throne to become a monk. Most of his relatives began with C: Clovis, Clothilda, Childebert. I'm glad he was not hung upside down, or roasted, struck by rocks or skewered by arrows.

You say you are now on the bottom rung of the tennis ladder, to your amazement. Of course you are not yet fit to play doubles: you have a lot of meat-eating to catch up. I'm amused that you have fitted yourself out with all the proper paraphernalia, down to frilly knickers and a new racquet press. I think I could enjoy it in slightly raised skirts and motoring hats, secured with tulle. Very small steps as one went to the net and a compromising curve of bust during service.

I hope you are feeling less uneasy about meeting his mother. Regard her as something inside brackets: a possibility, a cogitation. I remember that as the charm of algebra: its little parcels come complete. How beautiful brackets are when you think of them: in some typefaces the designer must have thought so, because they curve like arms.

I wish now I had paid more attention to your subject at school because it seems, like railway wagons, pieces of an argument can be uncoupled and a simpler solution found.

St Cloud seems a pleasing saint, don't you think? In my case the cloud of unknowing: had I been able to see the future I should never have lain with my head under a tap at the tennis courts with the water running straight into my mouth. I think that was the day a gesture indicated we would never be seriously watched again. But I mustn't blame myself entirely: I think you egged me on and tried to drink out of one of my tennis shoes.

A saint can't believe in clouds of glory: that would be too presumptuous. Just clouds.

Alice

St Ethelburga of Barking

Beatrix,

Wie geht's?

You sound more doubtful having met his mother. Perhaps you were right to regard this as crucial. Do you remember the Thom Gunn poem where this tug of war is sensed?

> *Two strangers left upon a bare top landing*
> *I for a prudent while, she totally.*

You say his mother passed between you and her son after he had opened the door to you and she was carrying a low bowl of hyacinths which were anchored by netting and flat stones. You may be reading too much into this. Though it was undoubtedly symbolic, it may not have been deliberate. And you wonder if she will care to part with such a fit young man who besides playing tennis can box and do jujitsu. If he mentions elopement as the only solution, it must be because he shares the same fears.

But if you elope what will become of your algebra? Will you both be able to return to St Hilda's? Or can you elope in the holidays? I don't wish to be gloomy but may it not end rather tamely, perhaps with you both living with his mother? I hope I am wrong but I've been saying 'elopement' and 'atonement' over and over in my head like a chant.

I'm going to give my paper after all. Even the professor is smiling at me. I must give another dinner party before I leave and perhaps this time, because of my preoccupation, there will be a need to introduce either Dreyfus or Garibaldi. But I hope not.

                                                        Alice

                        St Ursula the Unprepared

Beatrix,

Wie geht's?
   I'm flying tomorrow which means, since I am moving about, I shall miss your outcome. I can see these saints' names have been no help. When there is something real to be settled one becomes aware of the gap between an action, any action, and the written word. You say algebra is an artifice but so is language, speech, looks. You may have had your fill of all three by now and retreated into silence. Because I really believe that is the only alternative.
   But I hope it is not that. As algebra is mathematics in the guise of language — I had a sudden vision of a soft dress falling in folds — may you have the best of all worlds: sweet words and easy silences. And on a love-seat made for two.

                                                        Alice

P.S. I really believe there is something immature about eloping.

St John Southworth
Westminster Cathedral

Beatrix,

Wie geht's?

I've just seen a *real saint* and he's not at all as I supposed.

There was an Italian woman on the bus and it transpired we were going to the same place, though for her it is her parish church. Except it looks like a giraffe or something. A collection of Turkish rugs hung over a clothes-horse. A red brick university in revolt.

'You must see our saint,' she said. She was already winding a scarf over her head so St Paul wouldn't see her hair.

'I'll show you,' she insisted, as we went up the steps towards the giraffe. We could have been climbing the pink and white terraces.

Why is it we say we love plainness and would prefer to sleep on a futon and have a single chrysanthemum in a black lacquer vase and then when we see the Byzantine for the first time we lie on our backs with our legs in the air like dead spiders? That's how it felt, looking up.

The instant we got inside the doors the Italian woman started acting as though she was in a play, crossing herself and speeding up the aisle. But she had time to hiss at me in one of those carrying whispers: 'Left aisle, behind the rail.'

I didn't look down at first. Everywhere but down. The chapel roof and then the feretory roof and then my eyes fell on a pair of very slender feet, feet one felt had been stretched and taut, in love or waking or a last breath. Feet about size AAA in fine black woollen socks. I couldn't get over it.

'All he had to do was keep silent,' the lawyer I dined with

in London said. We had passed a captured car on the way to the restaurant, its wheels locked in a Denver clamp. As much chance as that. The judge wept because John Southworth was seventy. And then I suppose he was processed. Like scooping a fish in a net and killing it. Those wonderful socks. And the hands and face covered with a thick gold-plated mask.

Further along there was a Book of Remembrance. I decided to sign my parents' names in it and sat with a middle-aged woman on a bench. A very devout woman was bent over the book, inscribing a tribe of relatives. Then fifteen minutes went by and the woman beside me murmured she had to go and get her husband's meal. Finally I went and stood alongside the woman. Her little shopping cart was parked by the lectern and she was not adding names at all, but drawing. Scrolls and butterflies and swans. Daisy chains, briary roses, lovebirds. Someone called Smith had a swan with ripples and a bulrush. I asked if I could add my names and have her decorate them. 'What would you like?' she asked, biting the top of her pencil. 'I could do birds in a nest.'

Finally I couldn't find the exit and had to ask a young priest. He seemed to find the question amusing, but I really felt as though I was in the belly of a whale.

Wie geht's? How horrid. Someone in the crowd might have asked. There's no harder thing than being the centre of attention and fully conscious of it at the same time. Don't you think? Not grace through a hole in the wall, but grace observed. Wie geht's? Wie geht's? And no one, concentrating, can ever answer.

Alice

The Mask of Keats 🐦

When Nancy, in company with Fyodor, had crossed Tottenham Court Road and penetrated the cold and oddly unglamorous — though it may only have been the afternoon — streets that lie under the Post Office Tower, coming on the actress's flat suddenly and from a new angle, she felt all the ridiculousness of her errand and at the same time a ridiculous sense of loss.

'Keep Keats under the bed? Why, isn't he good enough to lie in it?' her friend had laughed on the telephone. Then she assured Nancy it wouldn't be the slightest bother, that she would not even disturb his dust.

'He can lie there like Quentin Crisp, wrapped in thoughts of Fanny. Wasn't he buried with Fanny's letters on his breast?'

But Nancy was jealous of her knowing even this much. She had not thought of the letters, white to match the mask, and she was discovering, thanks to Keats's travels, that jealousy can be jealousy of a journey.

Fyodor hadn't seemed to find the errand preposterous: tomorrow Nancy would go north on a coach and Keats would be endangered in her luggage, better for him to be boarded out. He stood behind Nancy as layer after layer of soft plastic was unwound: two Marks and Spencers' bags swathed like towels and the topmost one from Harrods. In the hollow where the real face had breathed very shallowly and the eyes were tightly closed — the only feature his sister Fanny found unlike — Nancy had packed a shredded *Guardian*.

The actress traced her finger down the slightly Roman nose and then, catching sight of Nancy's expression, suggested Mr Keats be shown his bed and they all repair to the sitting room for a glass of wine.

Half an hour later, when Fyodor and Nancy stood in the cold street, the actress hugged them both and promised, hands ridiculously crossed on her breast, 'not so much as a flirtatious look'.

'I'll inspect his lips for smudges when I get back,' Nancy had called over her shoulder. 'Don't you dare touch him.'

Hampstead, on her first visit, had hardly seemed to rise because Nancy was looking for nature, not houses. The Grey Green bus came to a halt outside what looked like a transport cafeteria, where other drivers were having tea or a smoke. A girl with a flower stall directed her, so on subsequent visits she plunged off like a homing dog or Keats himself with the thought of his little narrow bed, from whose stool he must have leapt like someone on a rebounder.

Nancy walked slowly about Keats's garden, keeping to the paths, in a quite different manner from the way she walked on to the heath, following a man with two dachshunds. And right up to Keats's gate she had walked with the determined tread of a Barbara Pym girl coming home from the office.

But once inside the gate her steps had become funereal, self-conscious, and when the first American student arrived, slowing equally, as though coming into harbour, they had conversed in near whispers.

'The £7 head,' Nancy said, trying to hide her excitement, to the shop assistant, who had laryngitis, so both their voices were lowered. The £14 head had a neck and base and might have sat on a piano.

'I think it is the last we have,' the assistant croaked. 'I'll have to take it out of the display case. But as you are a serious student . . .'

The other serious students had gone straight upstairs to the library to use the microfiche and look through magnifying glasses at the poet's not altogether easy hand. Only Nancy had behaved like a nation of shopkeepers.

The box was beautifully packed, so it need never be opened, and there was even a loop to insert her fingers. It swung easily like a lamp. But when she came to the corner and turned into the undulating cobbled street of North End Green, Nancy forced herself to stop smiling like a hallowe'en lantern and concentrate as one did in the heart of London, gripping one's handbag tightly. 'Act naturally,' she admonished herself. 'Pretend it is a cabbage or a vase. Take Keats for a coffee.'

> Walking through Bloomsbury
> With Keats's head in a box
> Fresh from the Keats Museum
> The expression his sister liked.

'Would you mind awfully if I joined you?' It was a plump middle-aged Englishman, tweedy and well cared for, with a faint blondish moustache.

When Nancy agreed readily, she was questioned, as she had come to expect, about her accent, her line of work, and how long she was intending to stay. Just like a customs official, she thought, but it was all completed in a few phrases. Then, as if reassured, they began to talk about the Heath and Nancy was able to question him about the rise of Hampstead, which had been obscured from the bus, partly by nervousness and partly by impressions from nineteenth-century books. Having fields replaced by buildings was perhaps enough to throw anyone.

'Oh the contours are there,' Colonel Wildermoth explained — he had introduced himself gallantly at the end of the little interrogation. 'Surely you must have noticed a rather steep protracted hill before you came down again on to the Green? Were you perhaps looking for a view of London from some hill? You need to go a distance on to the Heath for that.'

'It hardly seems like the Vale of Health,' Nancy said. In Camden Town she had looked down on the very seat where she and the actress had sat, escaping from the press of Camden Lock market, and eaten an enormous yellow doughnut with a red arterial spot of raspberry jam, and drunk coffee from paper cups. After that had come narrow darkened streets, large shabby houses with skips in their yards, a blackened church with vacant windows and some leafy side streets with doll-like houses, very like Keats and Brown's house itself.

Instead of looking for the underlying landscape in the landscape that had disappointed, she had looked for a short purposeful figure travelling at a measured pace, with a poem's metre.

After the colonel had gone, with much gathering up of walking stick, mackintosh and gloves, his seat was taken almost immediately by a woman of about forty-five with a lined, interesting face and shoulder-length lank hair touched with grey. She looked at Nancy for a few seconds, then asked if she could confide something.

'To a stranger, you understand. The way one confides something in a train. I just wanted to tell someone I've found out today I haven't got cancer of the nose. I've just been to the surgeon and got the results.'

'Oh how wonderful,' said Nancy. 'Can I buy you an extra cup of coffee or something to celebrate?'

'No, that's what I want to do for you. Would you like a muffin?'

'No, just a cappuccino would be fine.'

'I shall have to be careful, of course,' the woman confided when she was seated again, smiling and touching the bridge of her nose lightly to indicate the place to Nancy. 'I shall have to stay out of the sun and never go without a hat. I've decided to cancel going to Italy this year.'

'That's a shame,' said Nancy. 'Do you like Italy?'

'Adore it. But I'll gladly make the sacrifice. It was only when the surgeon told me, I realised I was thinking of it as a death knell.'

'And now, though everything's the same, it seems different?'

'I'm so glad I told you,' the woman said. 'Are you sure there is nowhere I can drive you? I took the rest of the day off, in case the news was bad.'

Nancy thanked her, but assured her she was where she wanted to be. She didn't admit she'd got on a bus going to Putney first because, once again, she had waited on the wrong side of the road. Had been surprised to find herself going over Waterloo Bridge, then pleased because there might be a glimpse of St Thomas's Hospital.

> *Keats in a box on the bus*
> *The front of the double-decker*
> *Travelling where he walked*
> *In every inclement weather.*

It was freezing when Nancy and Fyodor got back to London House and they had a cup of tea in his room. It was almost time for dinner in the vast monkish academic dining room with its dyspeptic portraits. Oils only moderately well done always transferred ill health to the sitter.

'Do you think that, Fyodor?' she asked. 'That oils are somehow a gauge of health?'

Haydon had done Keats like a romantic sardine, autumn-coloured, with his mouth slightly open. The authorities, seeing a video, would have asked, 'Who was that passionate red-haired fellow?'

Daisy, the dachshund, was a natural laggard and her owner had to stop frequently. Nancy brought up the rear, then made some general remarks about dogs. Sometimes she wondered if the frequency of them was for conversation starters. They walked on companionably past the Mixed Bathing Pond and towards Kite Hill. Other dogs were bounding about among the leaves and a groundsman was picking up papers with a stick.

'Is the Heath really safe?' Nancy asked her companion after a while. 'You hear stories . . .'

'Perhaps it never was. Safe enough by daylight, I should think. Armed with two dachshunds.' Daisy had gone off into a bush and they had to wait.

'I was thinking of a long time ago, when all this land was fields and London in the distance. The house I've just visited, Keats's House, is full of lithographs of Hampstead as it was in 1800. Now it looks as though it's been built up for centuries.'

'It used to be a weekend spa. It doesn't seem like it now. It's just as polluted as anywhere.'

'Someone said Hampstead is not so desirable. Oh Hampstead, they said. As though it was full of self-deluding snobs.'

'The place to live now is on the banks of the Thames. It's going to be another Venice.'

There was a tall, distinguished-looking man looking at Keats's bed on Nancy's second visit and she stood alongside him reading Keats's intimation of illness on the night of 3rd February, 1820.

Bring me a candle, Brown, and let me see this blood. I know the colour of that blood — it is arterial blood — I cannot be deceived in that colour — that drop of blood — it is my deathwarrant — I must die.

It was not 'blood' that stood out but *this* and *that*.

'It seems such a narrow bed,' Nancy said to the stranger 'and Keats was very short.'

'About five foot one, I believe,' the man replied.

They stood conversing for several minutes, side by side, without eye contact, like two mourners at a drive-in funeral viewing parlour.

'I suppose Brown might have helped him on the occasion of the spot of blood.'

'I don't imagine he felt much like leaping that night.'

The white coverlet and the sprigged green bed-curtains suddenly looked very cold.

'I haven't so much as kissed him,' the actress swore. 'Though he has got a nice mouth. I expect he did a fair amount of that himself.'

'Fanny in the bushes on the heath. And a fair bit in the poems. Everything seems to have touched him on the skin.'

'You'll find him under the bed where you left him.'

'Thanks,' said Nancy, when she saw he was safe.

'Besides,' said the actress, 'I've had Gaston staying. And he's more than half a head.'

Camden Town was hateful, even if Wentworth Grove was in the borough.

'The houses here are selling for half a million,' the actress had explained, as they tramped towards the market on their way to the tube to Bounds Green. Nancy held the actress's bag while she disappeared into an underground loo. She leaned against a Scottish bank offering loans to those with an established credit record.

The Lock was filthy and the press of black-coated bodies made it impossible to see the stalls. They had found the outdoor café with its window servery in gratitude and sank on to two miraculously vacated wobbly chairs in front of a table awash with Coke. But the doughnuts with their yellow centres and a violent spurt of jam were a joy. Soon their chins were covered with icing sugar. They could both have managed another but the queue was too long.

On her third visit to Keats's House, the contours of Hampstead had become clear. Ignoring the blackened wasteland of Camden, Nancy had perceived the swell of Belsize Park and the long hill near the Royal Free Hospital. Sitting in the back of the bus, painting her fingernails, one fingernail at each stop, she found she could think of it from a walker's point of view, replacing the tall gentrified houses with trees, feeling for the slopes where hay might have been forked until dusk by maidens and men.

'You need a toy boy,' the actress said, as they were picking their way between piles of litter on the way back to the Bounds End tube. The house where they had had a late lunch was propped up with scaffolding: it had permanently lost its balance during the Blitz. The squatters — a group of actors and musicians — had received orders to evacuate; as a last gesture they had prepared an elaborate feast on a door frame on two trestles, covered with a sheet.

One of the actors, who was thin-lipped, wore a beret which he never removed. He had once played the part of Trotsky.

'Young Trotsky, of course. Before he got axed.'

'Old Trotsky would be outside your range, I should think,' said one of the others, not unkindly. 'You're very good at young revolutionaries.'

It was dark in the front room due to a low-watt bulb and the scaffolding combined with the overgrown garden seemed to make the revolutionaries within even more reckless. We could be at Leigh Hunt's, Nancy thought, only would Leigh Hunt's wife have burnt the potatoes? The kitchen was upstairs at the back of the house and the meal was very uncoordinated.

When it was time to leave, the actress and her toy boy embraced passionately in the doorway, while Nancy stood under the arch of a hedge.

'It's useless looking for older men,' the actress said, kicking a McDonalds box with her boot. 'But a toy boy can be very sweet.'

It had been sweet, in another sense, walking through Regent's Park where the order was so dishevelled: perhaps this was the meaning of a toy boy, someone who woke looking rumpled and still beautiful? A breeze moved the fountain from its bowl and shaggy dogs spread the leaves. The walkers all looked resolute as though knowing they belonged to the wrong century; only a few lovers lingered in an exaggeratedly slow way, spoiling the effect in shabby coats. Nancy and the actress plunged down the middle path as though rushing to a king's levée and if there had been a maze, they would have been through it like retrievers.

A matter of days later, with a speed that would always delight her, Nancy was walking with two toy boys around Greenwich and talking about United States foreign policy. Fyodor was a student at the LSE and Willard a military historian writing a thesis on Russian-American relations. They had met, each carrying a tray, at dinner at the same long table and under the same kindly portrait who seemed to be regarding their little dishes of chicken Kiev and bread-and-butter pudding as a subsidy well spent.

One shared table led to another, with sometimes Fyodor and sometimes Willard, but it was pleasing, if one caught the other's eye, in the queue, or walking absent-mindedly past, thinking, in Willard's case, over his tutor's latest non-committal Brit remark, how readily they came together.

'Don't know what to make of the Brits,' Willard would say, stirring a fork into his beef Stroganoff as though looking for Russian submarines.

'I try not to come on too strong. So far he's given me three sentences, all neutral. Beats me how these people ever got up the steam for war.'

'I shouldn't underestimate them,' said Fyodor, stirring with his spoon at rice pudding with raisins. 'They've seen it all before. They don't need a lot of Yanks with nylons telling them how to run things.'

At Greenwich they had searched quite a long time for a teashop and Willard had mistakenly been given coffee in a tiny demi-tasse. He had gone back to complain while Nancy and Fyodor rolled their eyes and gave Gallic shrugs.

In the evenings they drank in the bar at Willy G and on some nights they sympathetically drank Coke.

If only the actress could see me now, Nancy thought, as she walked between them along a gravelled path near the

Observatory. Admittedly the subject was not very personal — the Cold War — but taking into account their ages (at least ten years younger) and their unforced presence, it did seem she had two toy boys of her own.

Keats, she recollected, had had such a relationship with Isabella, though Isabella was associated with fusty rooms, while Fyodor and Willard had seemed positively anxious to take a barge down the Thames. There is something gentle and undemanding in an older woman, she thought, praising herself now, since they were unlikely to, for drinking Coke and listening to Willard's descriptions of military families in small towns. She had encouraged his conservatism the way Isabella had encouraged Keats to begin a new poem, even lightly sketching the outline. Words like *honour* and *esprit de corps* — it could be the poet writing so many lines a day — came to her lips and were lightly taken up. When she turned her mind back to the conversation — they were passing the figurehead of the ship *Lysander*, a head entwined with snakes — the subject had changed to the plantation houses of Louisiana.

It is the ingenuous appeal of toy boys, Nancy thought, and if the actress had not had a toy boy of her own, she might have resurrected Keats from under the bed. Blown lightly on his face like someone blowing dust off a painting or a letter. In the end she decided they were not really toy boys at all: mere confidants through propinquity.

Walking rapidly through the London streets towards Willy G and afternoon tea, they had reverted to being three chilled individuals.

'What have you got there, luv?' the taxi driver asked, when she got back to Oxford Street and refrained from catching the flyer to Russell Square. Not that it was a flyer, more like a very tired old dromedary. Keats must have a ride in a taxi. She was going to say a cake or a hat. 'A head. The head of Keats.'

'Not alive, I hope,' said the driver. 'We get some strange things in the back of cabs. He's not alive, this Keats, I hope.'

'A life mask. Taken while he was alive, as opposed to a death mask, but no, he's dead. Died in 1821.'

'That's okay then. He can travel on the seat. Bit like carrying someone's ashes. We get that sometimes.'

> *Keats in a box in a taxi*
> *Leaving a generous tip*
> *'What you got there, luv?*
> *Better not ask, I expect.'*

Would Fanny Brawne have carried Keats's ashes, if she had them, in a hackney coach? Nancy wondered. It seemed not impossible. With both arms around them when no one was looking, just as he hadn't opened her last letters.

When the taxi pulled up at William Goodenough House, Nancy pressed a pound coin into the driver's hand and extracted the box carefully.

'Take care of him,' the driver called. 'Not often one gets such a well-behaved gent.'

Dear Keats, Nancy thought, I think I am beginning to understand. The taxi driver's remarks, meant kindly, had plunged her into depression again, as though only Keats could applaud himself or say when he was happy. It was no use telling him to cheer up; the plaster hadn't wiped out the spot of blood.

Back in her room at Willy G, as it was called by the long-term residents, those with two-bar heaters in their rooms and a strip of carpet which they bartered, Nancy put the box down on her blue quilt. It seemed a pity to break the string and the intricate noose. But the box was too deep for her suitcase and would have to be repacked.

Inside were layers and layers of paper and then straw. The hollow back of the mask was full of bubble paper.

She lay the mask gently on her bed and stroked the nose tentatively with one finger. The eyes stayed shut but the mouth was already sufficiently smiling.

'Ten minutes, Keats,' Haydon might have called. 'Can you stay still that long?'

'I can stay dead as long as you like. If I fall asleep, you can shave me.'

'I expect it feels like snow.' That was Severn, who was already beginning a sketch.

'Get on with it, Haydon, there's a good fellow. I want to go for a walk later.'

Then there must have been silence, or so it seemed under the plaster. The murmurs in the garden were blotted out and the warm plaster felt as if it was filling his lungs. It could have been plaster or it could have been earth.

Sensing this, someone, for a moment clutched his hand.

On the Gatwick Express, with Keats beside her in his blue overnight bag, an unpleasant fight had broken out between an elderly man and a conductor over a ticket. The old man had stood up and threatened to put up his fists. The train was travelling at an erratic speed so the idea of boxing was absurd. Some Americans in the carriage smiled and the man beside Nancy smiled and looked at his watch. When the fracas was over, a steward came through the carriage taking drink orders but nobody responded.

Keats had fought for over an hour with a boy who was tormenting a kitten: about the length of time it took the Gatwick Express to reach the airport. On either side of the tracks were groves of russet spindly trees and sometimes a High Street shot under them with its sample of English life: a pub sign, a taxi and a red bus.

It was the nose that was the problem. The nose that was trying to breathe.

Even under her feet in the plane, swathed inside the carry bag, she could feel the nose through her feet. She thought of the pinched noses of flat-on-their-bier kings, icy and sharp as razors, as though Death had maliciously added a peg. Breath was where the ice began.

A mask of Keats, Nancy had written on her Customs Declaration an hour before landing. And she had gone through the Agricultural Door as a ruse, since it was supposed to be quicker, by declaring '2 mulberry leaves and a sprig of laurelstine from Keats's garden'. The leaves and the laurelstine were pressed between the pages of the *London A-Z*.

'I expect they are well and truly dead,' the customs official said. 'But we'd better have a look, just in case.'

How was she going to write with the mask of Keats looking at her?

A single look and I should be wiped out, she thought. Even if it was a look of not knowing where he was, or which century. We close the eyes when we want to see the soul, not the other way around. Eyes show the moment, the tempo, the *vivace* or *legato* seconds. They show too much and they reveal almost nothing. Better the undisturbed lace curtains, the bamboo blinds.

In sleep the face looks most passionate, if it is passionate, or cold, if it is cold.

Above the thesaurus and the *Penguin English Dictionary* Keats hung like a white lamp. There are those who are luminous while they work or shortly after they have delivered: all the features of the mask had an extravagance that might be luminosity. Haydon had wanted him for a firebrand; lying motionless for the mask to set had not dampened the features: hair, eyeball and closed mouth were all that were necessary. And hadn't Brown said Keats's was the most ingenuous face ever seen?

> *Keats on a knot on my finger*
> *Keats in cut paper and straw*
> *Keats inside cardboard covers*
> *Keats breathing forever more.*

The Long Aunts &

Certain it became while we were still incomplete
There were certain prizes for which we would never
> *compete;*
A choice was killed by every childish illness,
The boiling tears among the hothouse plants,
The rigid promise fractured in the garden,
And the long aunts

> — W. H. Auden, 'A Bride in the 30's'

When my aunt Ada was dying, the priest came and pronounced she would recover. Five Protestant sisters waited in the hall, sceptical. They were even more sceptical in the bedroom where Ada slept, her beautiful wide forehead under an etiolated crucifix, a rosary twined over the bedpost and a small cut-glass dish of water and a hand towel beside it on the night table.

Ada kept a General Store where the main street widened and formed a half-crescent, like the edge of a lake. This impression was heightened for me by the boardwalk that ran outside and along which our feet clattered. Geese could not provide such a good alarm. Ada's private windows — the store was at one end — were hung with lace curtains so rich and baroque that her becoming a Catholic was only incidental. Secure in faith she slept with her windows open and the curtains moved in the moonlight like breath.

My mother, Irene, had saved nine shillings for a coat of

dove-grey material. She kept the sinks of the house in Royal Terrace where she worked spotless, as her mistress was prone to raids. When they went overseas and she was in charge of the household finances, she kept beautiful columns of expenditure. What can make the heart beat more than a possession to a saver? Not only a possession but a coat, to which she had added, long before de Beauvoir, her chosen range of selected images: sand and river stones when they are dry and dawn mist on wet fields. She carried it, panting a little, up Pitt Street with one finger stroking, through a hole in the paper, something that felt as soft and warm as feathers.

My brother and I rattled along Ada's boardwalk and boldly climbed on to a stool to peer into the freezers. The ice cream scoops rested in their sterilising jars but their capacities seemed limited to us. There was only so much a cone could hold without bursting. We built, with our lips between our teeth, towers of alternating flavours: strawberry, hokey pokey, vanilla. The scoops returned to their resting places, tired. Aunt Ada's son, Daniel, threatened to put locks on the freezers.

For my father I was copying details from a car manual into a stiff-covered notebook. I used a mapping pen and black mapping ink. The down strokes were as fine as hairs. I worked on it for half an hour each day, like a developing novelist. Sometimes, using baking paper, I traced a small diagram and drew arrows with feathered tails to the names of parts. But the book was not going as I expected; it was meant to look monkish: *The Carburettor* had exaggerated capitals and an extravagant slope. I threw my pen against the wall and dropped off the verandah and began to circle the house.

I'd been reading *Girl of the Limberlost* and the tussock reminded me of butterfly bog country. So silent was my approach I didn't see my brother or his strange, frozen, pleading posture until we almost collided at the verandah's end. Then the screen door banged and Aunt Jane appeared, sucking out of us any motion we might have dared contemplate by her fury, as she wielded the broom on the small brown snake that lay between us. I think she said, 'Keep still!' and we recognised it as something separate, like night and day, or north from south, as she swung and swung. Later she brought us glasses of lemonade on the verandah, where we sat bravely swinging our legs well above the ground. We swung in superiority to the snake that lay where the broom had tossed it, writhing, though technically dead, Aunt Jane said, until the sun went down.

In Aunt Ada's shop rakes and twine mingled with scent and dresses, colouring books with mousetraps, lengths of garden hose with talcum and moth balls. At a lower level, it seems, closer to the board floors, were the comestibles: the deep freezes with the already explored but not exhausted ice-cream compartments, the bacon slicer, individual cakes under a cupola of gauze. Aunt Ada, though no one had instructed her, was a natural book-keeper, taking the heavy ledgers back with her to the lace crucifix bedroom, where she sat working on them by the light of a small tulip lamp. She was also, it transpired, a female Robin Hood, a Manichee dividing profit from credit but seeing in the red charge columns of the truly desperate something deeper than red ink: blood. She counted: eggs, buns, an extra cake lifted with tongs, carelessly in the case of the poor and struggling but rigorously exact to make a proper dozen for the rich. There were no signs in her shop, except price tags, but if she had written one — she had quite fair copperplate — it might have read:

IF YOU ARE RICH DO NOT ASK FOR CREDIT.
EVEN THE RICH MAY BE OFFENDED BY A REFUSAL.

We are driving in the *Blue Flash*, a strange midnight-blue car with a wooden steering wheel and bits of upholstery hanging from the roof. It is like driving underwater or being in an endless Ghost Tunnel. Aunt Jane's husband, Frank, is driving. The landscape is blue as well; everything exudes blueness or matches blueness. Suddenly two large kangaroos come straight out of the bush and cross the road in front of us. Their pace doesn't slacken and they have a single-minded look, in profile.

'The mail,' says Uncle Frank.

'Mail?' we shout, in unison.

'Letters and parcels. The big one has the parcels and the little one the letters. I thought you knew.'

We look at his adult eyes reflected in the driving mirror but their expression seems normal. Even the lines around them haven't moved.

My mother spends three weeks in Melbourne's most glamorous hotel, Menzies, looking after two American children. She has a suite on the top floor, room service and someone to put coal on the fire at regular intervals. Her sisters, Rose, Eileen, Ismay, crowd into the suite and roll their eyes. Irene orders tea. She is becoming blasé, knows it, and will do nothing about it. The American children are delightful and her employers wish they could keep her. Every morning a taxi takes my mother and the children to the park or zoo and brings them home again. The children watch the animals and my mother watches the children.

Years later she still says, 'Those Americans!' This may be where my love of hotels begins.

The suitors of my aunts nearly came to blows. Not once but several times. Six sisters meant you could pick a sister in reserve if your first proposal was rejected. Jane's husband had my mother second. My father had Jane. Flattery and bad taste are strange bedfellows. How dare a first choice become a second? The sisters were questioned: 'Would you have taken X if I had not come along?' It left a residual unease for years. If X, Y, or Z had asked first, would she have had the good judgement to wait? Only Eileen never married. Her fiancé died in the war and she kept his photo to ward off shoppers with lists.

Uncle Stanley, married to Rose (*her* second choice), lit cheroots from a kerosene lantern on the long scrubbed table. Hams, onions and puddings in strange cloths, like sheets pulled over the heads of the dead, hung from the pantry ceiling. Huge red Aberdeen Angus bulls were branded while the women stayed indoors, a kind of purdah, though they wore print afternoon dresses. A hundred yards of dogs, with a greyhound at the head, were released to chase rabbits at sundown. Rabbits with tails like mull sticks would make the land thrum.

By day the house was cool: its thick walls could have been carried by an iceman on a bicycle. *The iceman cometh* was one of my favourite sentences. The whole perimeter, with its overhanging verandah, had French doors, regularly spaced. The rooms were plain and, once you got used to them, wholesome. Each tiny feature: a door clasp, a curlicue of wrought iron, stood out. In a field outside, Uncle Rupert, Stan's brother, kept a killer horse which reared.

My mother, in white uniform and white apron (afternoons were black uniform, white apron), walked down 58 steps at 5.30 a.m. The noise of the lifts might have woken the Governor. The maids separated and began to clean out the ashes and black-lead the fireplaces. My mother weighed little over seven stone and was lucky to get the job. Margo, the housekeeper, a red-haired Scotswoman, as haughty in her own way as the butler, asserted that small maids were often the best workers. My mother's glowing references instantly grew wings at each corner; when she repacked them, they fluttered and bumped inside her trunk.

When the Duke and Duchess of York came to Government House, Margo fretted about the possibility of leaking hot-water bottles. Alex, who shared a room with my mother, had self-confessed weak wrists. But my mother, delicate in everything else, had wrists that could have been designed for wringing chickens' necks or pitching baseballs. 'Irene screwed them on, Margo,' they would call to Margo's departing back and see her shoulders relax like a Citröen after someone has sat in it.

Rose sailed to Malta with two children; Eileen worked for a society doctor; Ada worked in the General Store with her husband, soon to die of undiagnosed appendicitis which became peritonitis. Irene nursed a society child with chicken pox who refused to sit in the front seat of a limousine with his mother, who was wearing a silver fox fur. 'It won't be the same without Reeny,' he sobbed. 'I'm not going anywhere without her.'

Then Irene and Eileen worked together: nanny and cook to a lovely couple who went to hear Gladys Moncrieff. The husband wore an evening cape and carried a cane, which Eileen handed to him — he was very handsome — with a mock bow. 'Do we look all right, I and E?' they would chorus, one dark and scarlet-tinged like neon and the other silver and breathtaking as a fish, as they swept out. Then the children could have extra sweets, two picks from the big jar, and I and E would sit at the kitchen table drinking cocoa until they returned.

Ismay sat on Irene's chest with a tomahawk in her hand. Ismay (10), Irene (6).

'You can come and say goodbye to her,' she shouted to Rose, Ada, Jane, Eileen, who came running. 'I'm going to cut off her head.'

One hand, in readiness, held Irene's throat level with the ground; already Irene's head felt half-buried, even to herself. The blades of grass seemed to spring and swell on either side. She felt like a fish in water, with side vision.

Ada and Eileen seized one each of Ismay's arms and Rose plucked the tomahawk.

'Beasts,' she screamed, but secretly relieved. Just where she was to lower the tomahawk she was uncertain. Would one stroke be enough for her sister or should she stun her first with the blunt side?

'Little savage. You should be ashamed of yourself.'

One of the sisters pushed Ismay so she landed face down on the grass. Irene was hauled to her feet and then on to someone's shoulders. Probably Eileen's, who was, besides the most peaceful, tallest.

'I'll get you. You needn't think I've forgotten . . .'

But already everyone was out of earshot. Bloodlust, even the feeble sisterly kind, became grass. Luxuriant springing memory.

Christopher, the eldest son of a Melbourne society doctor,

set to become a society doctor himself in two decades, had mumps and then measles. In his darkened room, dwarfed by fat pillows and a soft silk eiderdown like a woman's body, Irene was a square of light (her long French-waiter's-style apron) and a crescent (her cap). Sometimes, in his delirium, she seemed like a little white house, the sort his sister Louisa might draw; at other times, with the shadows on her apron, a window.

When he was well, he had a boiled sweet every evening from the big glass bottle with the stopper. Sometimes, pretending to choose, he held one in each hand, like an X-ray plate, hoping to keep both. Louisa, who was born without scruples, inserted a fist, scooped what she could hold, and made a dive for the nursery door. Irene caught up with her and prised her fingers apart, counting out the sweets: Wednesday, Thursday, Friday. By the time Christopher was a distinguished surgeon, Louisa had three divorces.

'How dare he know that she's not going to die,' Rose said, after the short plump priest had passed between them.

'Did you see how smug he looked?'

'Perhaps he forgot the holy water and this is his excuse.'

'Whatever it is, I don't care. As long as *she* believes it.'

'You know how broken-hearted father was when she turned.'

'As though he'd discovered a priest-hole behind the dresser.'

'Now Charlie's dead and she's left with all this.'

All this included what looked like a collection of bookmarks and postcards in Ada's handkerchief drawer, with prayers and messages to saints and some preserved sprigs of macrocarpa, though why these were distinguished no one could tell.

'At least there are no statues, like the Kingsley place. How Marianne can sleep in that room.'

Ada, opening her eyes slowly, saw their five Protestant faces in the doorway. None was admitting they had approached the handkerchief drawer or picked up one of the dried sprigs and sniffed it. Lovely as any keeper of priest-holes, she thought: the Protestant responsibility of building them and pushing someone into one, waving a huge cloak to cover a Stuart Pretender. She meant, though she could not marshal her thoughts, not just yet, that their clear high foreheads and serene waved hair were a moral act in themselves.

Rose, long before riches came to the long-windowed, veranda-encircled rooms, before the red scorched cattle and the posse of dogs, while they still had lanterns, left Frank and walked the nine miles to Ada's General Store. She carried a small cardboard suitcase with a label saying *Bushy Park* in which was packed an overlarge floral nightdress with a V neckline, a change of underclothes and a spare blouse, and Tolstoy's *Anna Karenina*.

There were no trains in O—— and in any case Rose was too exhausted to consult a timetable. She was strong and healthy, like all the aunts, but she foresaw a life of endless drudgery.

Ada, sitting up in bed, working on her accounts and calculating how many lamingtons and meringues she could afford to give away in a week, was at a loss for solutions. She swept the ledgers on to the floor and insisted Rose have her bed. Rose, to her surprise, accepted gratefully. The plainness of her own room receded. The lace curtains, so thick and clotted, their edges with holy medals clinging to them like minnows, produced an odd sense of happiness. The aspidistra in its burnished pot, the little line of African violets kept her company. She forgot the quarrel, which had been no worse than others, and was surprised in the morning by a footfall on the boardwalk and a rough hand bearing flowers.

Jane, whom my father had replaced by Irene, and Frank, whose list had my mother second, had one child, Reuben, a birth of legendary difficulty. My mother had two easy births and one miscarriage, after which she was seen by the specialist and reassured, as though she had been a good girl and not drunk gin or thrown herself down the stairs — two ideas that would never have occurred to her — that everything was perfectly fine. But he said it in such a way, as though releasing her from the slightest taint of suspicion, that she felt both praised and alarmed.

Jane's child was to be a prodigy since Frank had determined, and broadcast to anyone who would listen, that there would be no other.

In the summer of the snake and the laborious copying of the car manual, Reuben was up to a great deal of mischief which his parents failed to see, as someone with long sight may miss a foreground fog. Most of it had to do with a disused barn with an attic, and dressing up in women's clothes. Reuben in a silk dress and a black straw hat with absurd bunches of wine-coloured cherries. Reuben's green face smoking a cigar stolen from his father's rolltop desk. Reuben pulling the wings off moths before my brother or I could stop him.

I had felt nothing but exultation for the crushed-headed snake writhing in the dust and Aunt Jane pointing out its heart, 'six inches behind the head', like someone pointing out the very hole made by a small meteor. But everything else that summer was influenced by the thin up-and-down strokes of my fine mapping pen: the up strokes as tentative as a daddy-long-legs — Reuben had tortured one of those too, to see how many legs it required — and the down strokes more like the beat of arterial blood. Everything that summer had, for the first time in my life, a sharp uniqueness, capable of pain and pleasure, like a blade of grass.

Rose's daughter, Denise, before her wild talents found or created a rich conservatism, was famous for bluntness. In the little village where all the family, except my mother, lived, on farms or in the village itself — Ada's store was already a classic — huge logging trucks were often seen at dusk, some with a single log. The log passed as easily as a coffin on even shoulders or a bride gliding up an aisle. It was while one such log was passing that Denise, aged eighteen, with dark Heathcliffian looks and probably a wing of dark hair lightly lifted by the swoosh of the convoy, was accosted between two of a row of plane trees, almost the only attractive thing in the village, and asked for a date by a young man.

Her reply — dusk had sunk quickly into night, or her reply had prompted it — came like gunfire: 'I'd rather meet an alligator in the dark than go dancing with you.'

Then the suitor, as the huge log wound its way uphill, must have turned on his heel and walked away. And Denise was nowhere on anyone's list.

Fascination with genealogy is a lack in the self. How many nondescript, circumscribed lives rely on this inward-turning when it seems the world will never turn to them? Was there a pirate once in the family? A highwayman? A noble in a crumbling pile over whose herbaceous and topiaried beds bindweed and convolvulus make a veil? A circumnavigator, a botanist, a diarist? How did they spend time, who have left others so lonely, or did they, like vampires, expend the energy of their ancestors? The long aunts cast a shadow (approaching the summer house, overhearing the row — in this decade it would be heavy breathing — perhaps one would turn on the hose?) but they lived lives of perfect tactfulness. Though I sometimes burrowed deeply inside my scattered, and probably far from accurate memories of them, I felt no pressure to emulate.

Just keep breathing, they seemed to say. Ada had kept breathing and recovered without histrionics. They had all turned out well, that was the miracle my mother, who was prejudiced, claimed for them. It was the gossip of the village. Visiting from New Zealand, she was mistaken for one of her sisters when she took an evening walk. There were still suitors in the shadows and still the hint of lists.

My mother, 'married and gone to New Zealand', was the only sister, after the time when her sisters travelled as children's governesses, ladies' companions, to Malta, Burma, America — Rose went to New York but didn't leave the ship — to travel in her later life.

A poor sailor, she spent numberless Tasman crossings praying fervently for the ship to go down, while her husband, dismissed with a Mimi-like wave of the hand, strode the decks and ate heartily, alone. We thought her lack of logic appalling, amusing.

'Didn't you care about anyone?' we asked and she answered, 'No, not anyone.'

She was helped ashore with greenish cheeks and weighing a mere six stone. She never approached a ship if she could help it: a sight of a bow was enough to bring back the smell of the corridors, the oil and paint which was applied unhealthily, like layers of pancake. Before each crossing my father attempted to fatten her, like Hansel in the witch's cage, but each time she disembarked, her fingers were as thin as chicken bones.

Rose, Eileen, Irene and Ada. Here they are in a photograph rescued from an old box of photographs of family picnics, the arrival of the 'new' car, an oval-windowed Pontiac, myself in a suit with huge buttons down the back which imprinted me if I leaned against anything, holding our tabby cat, Tiger. In a large family — something I am imagining — the first born were married before the middle and later layers arrived. My mother's older sisters were aunts to her: Rose, Eileen, Jane, Ada, Ismay (of the axe) she was privileged to know. Ismay was on holiday when the photograph was taken and Jane was recovering from giving birth to the prodigy.

They are standing outside Rose's house, Willamette, where the kerosene lamps from which Stan and Rupert lit their redolent cigars have been replaced by electricity. Nothing is seen of Willamette but a piece of wall, one of the blank stretches between two French windows. Behind their feet is a small strip of garden, which from its burnt-off condition and their dresses indicates high summer.

I want to make them leap from the photograph for a moment: Ada and Rose with their noble, moon-like foreheads (I mean if moonlight touched those fine broad planes it would find an answering reflection). Eileen's and my mother's narrower, longer faces, the moon in its first quarters.

I must have been there that day, playing somewhere

beyond the lens — it might have been the day my brother borrowed the horse and enticed it to jump fences, a revelation that caused as much consternation as Uncle Stan imagined was attached to the branding of cattle. Behind me stretch the red cattle, the hills, the dogs running after rabbits.

I must have had the germ of an idea that day because seeing the photograph makes me realise how much this idea has held. In Rose's eyes I see the anguish and defeat of the suitcase, a beautiful and inexpressible nobility that you sometimes see in the expression of a white horse. Eileen, who stayed with my grandmother, Charlotte, rescuing her from floods and walking with her to church until she was confined to bed, has the look of a unicorn, a faraway and unconnected horn on her head. Ada, breathing in a Catholic way behind invisible lace curtains, her ledgers in as good order as her soul.

Watching them that day, probably writing in the dust, for my mother in her dress of large triangles has a look of wishing to reprimand — any moment now her waved head will turn and two dark eyes be fixed on mine — don't I know there is a water shortage? we are bathing in five inches like the King — I am making the cruel judgement of my father, of Frank and all the men. I am seeing them as cutouts, paper legs joined and hands held. Who takes what from whom? What is this knowledge outside *Burke's*? Now I have learned of Mendel's peas, I think they have beaten me even to that, deliberately designing their frocks from plain to swirls to triangles. Four is one and one is four, they seem to be saying, and if there is any anguish in their eyes it is at my obtuseness. Four is twelve or one is twelve. Or any number for that matter. Mendel scoops the gene pool with a net and four goldfish or four leaves are caught in the muslin.

But my mother and her sisters, my long aunts, backs against a blank wall, are saying something different. We are anarchists to everything you believe about us, they are saying. We are being shot, but we are still anarchists.